ROSE
COTTAGE

MARY STEWART

ROSE COTTAGE

DOUBLEDAY DIRECT LARGE PRINT EDITION

William Morrow and Company Inc.
New York

**This Large Print Book carries the
Seal of Approval of N.A.V.H.**

To the gentle shades of Henry, George, Patsy, Nip, Rosy, Maudie and Muffin, and all the other friends whom I met again in my stroll down Memory Lane.

1

It is 1947, a calm still day of June. On the wide spreading moorland the ling is dark and as yet unflowering, but the bell heather is out, and bees are busy. Sunday afternoon peace. A grouse calls somewhere, safe still for a few weeks from men and guns.

The weather has been fine, and the hillside is dry, but a little way down the slope the cotton-grass shows fluffy-white among the reeds and dwarf thickets of bog myrtle. A tiny burn drips and trickles down to where the bog water gathers in dark brown pools, to soak away gently towards the river that winds along the base of the strath.

Strathbeg, the valley is called on the maps, the small glen. To its few inhabitants it is just "the glen", and the big house, Strathbeg Lodge, to be glimpsed among its sheltering trees some way below, is simply "the House". Built originally as a shooting-lodge, it has belonged for some years to the Brandons, who used to come here each year in summer from their home in the north of England. From a distance the Lodge is imposing, with its baronial turreting and stepped roofing, its well-grown timber and its lawns reaching to the river with its series of salmon pools, but from nearer can be seen the signs of the neglect enforced by the recent war; the woodwork could do with a coat of paint, the rhones all too obviously need to be cleaned out, the lawns are no longer lawns, but pastures cropped by sheep. It is still not possible, two years after the end of the war, to find the labour and the materials necessary to restore the place to good order, but the family make the best of it, and the best, in fact, is very pleasant. After the traumas and shortages of the war years the glen is a haven of peace, and a steady supply of milk, eggs, fish, mutton and venison goes a long way to make up for threadbare carpets and unmended pipes and the eccentricities of the plumbing.

The family, what is left of it, came here to stay in 1940, when their English home was requisitioned by the RAF, Lady Brandon settled in with her married daughter and the daughter's two children. Sir James spent his war in London, only travelling north for brief leaves. The son, Gilbert, who was unmarried, was killed at El Alamein. Now that the war is over the son-in-law, Major Drew, is home, and taking over on behalf of his own small son, William, who is the heir. Sir James is home, too, but feels his age these days — he is well into his sixties — and the family seems to have settled happily enough into the quiet glen. Tod Hall, their home in England, having housed a series of high-spirited airmen dedicated to living the brief span of their doomed young lives to the full, has suffered so much damage that Sir James, without too much regret, has decided to use the compensatory cash to turn it into an hotel, and himself retire for good into the peace of Strathbeg. A peace which, at this moment, one could believe never to have been broken.

The burn, lapsing in whispers, is, apart from the bees, the only sound in the day. Both are drowned in the sudden *hear ye, hear ye* preliminary whistle of a curlew, and then the sky is filled, it seems, with the beautiful long, liquid call that is perhaps the loveliest, the most thrilling of all birds' songs. "The silver chain of sound" was how George Meredith described the lark's singing, and poet after poet has added praise to the nightingale; but it would take all the poets, from Wordsworth down, to do justice to the curlew's call. I, certainly, cannot describe it, other than to say that every time that liquid gold pours and bubbles through the sky, my skin furs up like a cat's and my throat tightens with tears.

This was the effect that the song was having on the young woman who sat near the brow of the hill. She sat at ease on the heather, apparently with no other thought than to listen to the curlew's song. She was a tall girl in her mid-twenties, dressed in a tweed skirt that looked expensive, and a silk shirt. Her hair was dark and fashionably cut, slightly ruffled in the shifting hilltop air. Her eyes — dark, too — were fixed on the curlew which, suddenly falling silent, was gliding to the heather some two hundred yards away. It would land, she knew, well short of its objective, and make a long and circuitous approach to the hiding-place of its lurking, all-but-invisible young. It had, while pouring out that glorious, heart-piecing song, most certainly had both beady eyes on her, and would be watching her still.

As the thought touched her, she saw the foolish, long-beaked head pop up against the skyline, then vanish again swiftly, as no doubt the scuttling babies were herded away to safety. She smiled, and with the smile her face — which in repose was perhaps too serious, too set with some sort of private effort at self-rule — lighted, as she had been told at various times that it did, to a kind of beauty.

As she had been told. As I suppose I may not say for myself, since the girl (who was getting to her feet and brushing the heather-dust from her skirt, in preparation for setting off downhill) was myself. Myself when young, some fifty years ago. Mrs Kate Herrick, aged twenty-four, widowed, well-to-do, and here in Strathbeg to visit her grandmother, who was employed as cook at the House.

Somewhere deep in the heather the grouse called again, "Come back! Come back!" And indeed Mrs Kate Herrick, who had been Hathy Welland, and who had helped in the kitchen and sometimes in the gardens of the House, had at last, and after more than four years, come back.

I looked at my watch. Gran would be awake now and, after the comings and goings of the morning, there would be time at last for that private talk. I had not arrived till late on the previous night, and still did not know why she had so urgently summoned me north "to have a real talk. No, not on the phone, hen, I'll tell you when you come." Then as an afterthought: "You do remember Rose Cottage, don't you?"

Of course I remembered Rose Cottage. It was one of the cottages on the Brandons' English estate, and lay some two miles from the village of Todhall. My grandfather as a young man had been a gardener at the Hall, and one summer, when the family (as the Brandons were locally known) went north to their newly purchased Scottish estate, he went with them, to help with the recovery and remaking of the long-neglected garden. There he met and fell in love with Mary Campbell, the kitchen-maid. They were married the following spring, in Todhall. A year later their daughter was born. In an uncharacteristically poetic moment they called her Lilias, a name taken from one of the portraits of long-dead Brandons that hung at the Hall. Lilias was my mother. I barely remembered her, but the memory was all delightful. Deliciously pretty, full of joyous spirits and invariably kind, she danced her way up from scullery-maid to the heights of house-maiding at the Hall with a light heart and, as was found to my cost, what her eighteenth-century namesake would have called a light skirt.

I had never been told who my father was. My mother was of course banished from service at the Hall when she was found to be pregnant. Her parents, defying the customs of the time, took her in, and cared lovingly for her and, in due time, for her baby, while the Brandons, without a word on the subject, left their gardener and their cook to manage their own affairs. Which showed their good sense, since cooks as good as my grandmother were even in those days hard to come by.

When I was five years old, my grandfather died. I could barely remember him; a comfortable, earth-smelling giant who when my mother was elsewhere used to take me up to the walled garden and let me play — "helping Granddad," he called it — in the back premises behind the glasshouses. Soon after his death Gran's elder sister came from Scotland "to keep her company". This was Aunt Betsy, and with her came change.

Aunt Betsy was religious. Her religion, which kept her very strictly in the paths of righteousness, also obliged her to see that other people trod the same thorny path. Things which had never been said before, were said now, and frequently. (So much I did hear, later, from my grandmother.) Rose Cottage was no longer a place of kindness, but of Godliness with a capital G. My mother stood it for a year, then one night, soon after my sixth birthday, she left.

The room I shared with her was at the front of the cottage, over the kitchen, which was our main living-room. I was wakened from sleep by raised voices. Gran's, urgent with something that could have been despair or anger. My mother's, unwontedly shrill and tearful. Aunt Betsy's, high, hard, and assured. I slid down under the bedclothes and covered my ears.

A door slammed. I pushed the blankets back and sat up. Light footsteps on the bare wooden stairs. My bedroom door opening softly. My mother at my bedside, arms tight round me. A hand coming gently to stifle my questions.

"It's all right, love. All right. Mummy's going away for a bit, that's all. Be a good girl now, won't you?"

"Where're you going?"

"Just away. Not far."

"Can't I come too?"

"No, baby, no. But I'll come home soon, see if I don't, and then old Sourpuss'll get her cards, and we'll all be happy again." A giggle, then a swift kiss, which let me know that there were tears on her cheeks. "I've got to go. Mind your books at school now, Kathy. You're a bright girl, and you'll go a long way. See it's a better way than me. Go to sleep now, lovey, and don't forget your mum." A quick hug and another kiss. "Good night, baby."

I stood at the window and watched her go down the front path. The moonlight was strong enough for me to see that she had Granddad's battered old Gladstone bag in one hand, and in the other a bulging bass carrier of the sort that the family used for game and salmon.

I never saw her again. She had gone with the gipsies, Gran said. Every year they came to the same lane near our house for a few nights, and they were there on the night she left. But by morning the camp had vanished without trace, and there had been no way of getting in touch with her. From time to time she wrote, usually with the cards she sent for Christmas and for Gran's and my birthdays. Some two years later she sent news that she was going to be married ("so tell the old cat") and was off to Ireland where "Jamie" had been offered a job. She would write from there and tell us all about it. But she never did. She had been killed in a bus crash, she and her Jamie, somewhere in the west of Ireland. That was all Gran told me; it was Aunt Betsy, inevitably, who gave me the details. The couple had been the only passengers in the small country bus, when, in the dark, it ran into a stray bullock loose on the road, and plunged down a bank and burst into flames. The driver, "a good man, though no doubt he was a Catholic", had been thrown clear, but had been badly burned himself in trying to free the two passengers. "And it was to be hoped" (this was Aunt Betsy again) "that they were dead already."

I do not know what Gran would have said if she had known about this, but, childlike, I said nothing, and took out my grief and horror in nightmares. But when, a little time later, Aunt Betsy was found to be working a text in cross-stitch which said THE WAGES OF SIN IS DEATH, my grandmother, normally the gentlest of women, tore it out of her sister's hands and threw it into the fire.

And for once Aunt Betsy never said a word.

2

When I was sixteen the war broke out. I was at the local grammar school. The only other girl from the village who went was the vicar's daughter, Prissy Lockwood. Our cottage lay almost two miles from the village, on the way to the station, and Prissy and I travelled together daily, two stops down the line. She was just about my only contact with the village in those days; there was very little to do in Todhall, and our relations with the Hall were hardly social. I worked there when I could — a shilling an hour — helping Gran in the kitchen. It paid my train fares, and helped a little here and there. At home I kept a good deal to my room, working most evenings at my schoolbooks, to keep out of Aunt Betsy's way. My great-aunt was a good housekeeper, and I am sure that she was a help to Gran, who was working most days away at the Hall, but I knew that she still re-

garded me as the offspring — and probably the inheritor — of Sin, and things
were never other than distant between us.
I sometimes caught her watching me with
what looked like positive dislike, but it is
impossible to be accurate about such
things, and her normal expression was, to
say the least, sour and forbidding. She
died in 1945, of a cancer that we had
never suspected, and which she bore with
the same ferocious strength that she had
brought to her fight against Sin. By that
time I had been away from home for
nearly five years.

In 1940 the Hall was taken over by the
RAF, and the family went north and asked
Gran to go with them. She went with few
regrets, her only worry being my future.
Aunt Betsy (who in fact had not been
asked to go) declined to leave Todhall;
Gran would be "living in" at Strathbeg
Lodge, and there were new tenants in the
Campbell cottage there, so Rose Cottage
must remain her home. Things looked
bleak for me. But here the vicar and his
wife intervened, having no doubt heard
something of my situation from Prissy. For
my final year at school I was to lodge at

the vicarage, and Prissy and I would take our Highers together. Which is what happened. My results were rather better than Prissy's, a fact which she accepted with cheerful indifference: she had never had any ambitions beyond marriage and a family, and in fact, after leaving school, she only put in a year with me at a teachers' training college in Durham before marrying a young officer whom she met on holiday, and relinquishing her college place without regret. I finished my course and was then — to my grandmother's delighted pride — appointed to an elementary school in a small Yorkshire town. I found lodgings near at hand, and, since I spent my holidays in Scotland, where I was glad to earn a little extra by "helping out" at the House, I saw nothing of Todhall for the next few years.

Of my marriage I will say little except that it was a typical war-time affair, too commonplace in those days to be seen as tragic. I met Jonathan Herrick at a concert given by Yehudi Menuhin. In those days the great artists travelled the country, taking music to out-of-the-way places, playing sometimes even in village halls. Jon and I had seats next to one another. We were both in uniform — he was a Flying Officer, and I did part-time war service in the Royal Observer Corps, and had just come off duty — and in the intervals we talked, and after the concert we went out together and sat for hours over ersatz coffee in some small bar-café. We met again, took a bus out into the country and walked and talked. I don't remember what about; he told me little of himself or his family, and nothing of his work; I knew merely that he was flying bombing missions over Germany. I took to watching and listening for the Halifaxes on "bombers' night", and, when I was on duty, painfully trying to track the numbers of aircraft going and returning, without ever knowing which missions he was on.

In a short time — time was precious in those days — and after a few more meetings, I found that I loved him. We married, a typically hasty war-time affair, at which not even Gran (who was temporarily back at Todhall nursing Aunt Betsy) could be present. Five weeks later, in the last months of the war, Jonathan was killed. I found, to my stupefaction, that he had been wealthy, the only son of well-to-do parents who were both killed when a flying bomb got their Sussex home in a direct hit. That, with all it had held, was gone, but there was a London flat, and a great deal of money, all of it apparently mine. No angry relative turned up to contest it; there was no one, and Jon, his lawyers told me gently, had been careful to make a Will a few days before we were married. So there was I, Kate Herrick (Jon had hated the name Kathy and never called me by it), wealthy, widowed, and quite content to throw up her teaching job just as soon as the war ended, and move to the London flat. Eventually, because I found it hard to do nothing, but had no desire to go on teaching, I went to work in a big plant nursery at Richmond, which was run by the widow of one of Jon's friends, whom I had met during the brief days of my marriage.

Then came Gran's telephone call.

I was working in the potting rooms behind the shop. We had just had a delivery of pot-plants, and I was unpacking them, when one of the young sales assistants came running in.

"Phone for you, Kate. Long distance, so hurry."

I set down the pots I was holding, and wiped my hands hurriedly on the tissue wrapping. "Who is it, do you know? The Dutchmen, I hope? Those bulbs should have been here a week ago."

"I don't think so. Moddom says it's private. It's in her office, and so's she." "Moddom" was the junior help's name for Angela Platt-Harman, the owner of Platt's Plants, and my employer.

"Oh dear," I said. We were not supposed to make or take private calls at work, but my apprehension was only a token, a kind of expression of solidarity with my co-employees. In the work-place Angie and I were always, carefully, employer and employed.

"It's all right, she didn't look mad." She hesitated. "I was in the office when she answered it, and she sent me to find you. It's Scotland. Doesn't your family live there? I hope it's not —"

I didn't wait to hear what she hoped it wasn't. I ran to the office.

Angie was speaking into the telephone. "No, it's no trouble. Quite all right, really. Ah, here she is now. Just a moment." She covered the receiver with her hand. "Kate, it's your grandmother, but don't worry, she says there's nothing wrong." She handed me the receiver and pointed me to the chair behind her desk. "Take your time. I'll see to the shipment." She went out of the office.

I sat down. "Hullo, Gran? How lovely to hear you. How are you? When they said it was Scotland, I was afraid there might be something wrong. Are you all right?"

"I'm well enough." It seemed to me, though, that there was a quaver in the old voice that told of some distress or urgency. "It's all a lot of fuss, nothing but a touch of flu, and you know how it goes to my stomach, and the fool of a doctor says I'm not to go back to work for a bit yet, but I'm fine now, and come the month-end I'll be back at the House. That Morag may fancy herself at the clootie dumplings and broth and such, but she's a lot to learn afore she can dress a fish properly, or put a dinner on when they've company."

"Don't you worry about that, Gran. They'll do all right at the House. Just get yourself better, that's what matters. But hang on a minute, I didn't know you'd been ill. What is it? You said stomach trouble? What does the doctor say?"

"Never mind that now. This is dear, phoning. I know I didn't ought to have called you at work, but I can't get to a phone in the evenings, and you and I've got to have a real talk, and not on the phone. What I wanted to ask you — Kathy, hen, when do you get your holidays?"

"When I ask for them. I'm due some time, anyway. Do you want me to come up now, Gran? Of course I will! I can look after you if you're supposed to rest. In fact I'd love to come. London's horrid in June. Can they have me? Will I be in my old room?" My room had been a small attic at the House, with no mod. cons., but with a breathtaking view over the whole length of the glen, right to the distant gleam of the sea-loch.

"No, didn't I tell you? I've got my own place now. I've got Duncan Stewart's house, down by the burnside. You'll mind the one, with the wee garden that used to be the kailyard."

"I remember it. How lovely! No, you didn't tell me."

"Oh, well, you know I'm not much of a hand at writing, and it's a long way to the post office for the telephone, and my legs aren't so good these days."

"Are you phoning from there now?"

"No, from the hospital. Now don't fret yourself, I'm going home tomorrow, and Kirsty Macdonald — you mind her, she has the house next door — says she can look after me fine. But there's something I want to talk to you about, Kathy love, and something I want you to do for me. It's important, and it won't wait. No, not on the phone, hen, the girls at the desk hear everything. It'll keep till you get here. It's about Rose Cottage — you do remember Rose Cottage, don't you? Well, then, can you really come?"

"Of course I can. I'll go and see the boss now, and I'll be with you some time at the weekend. Take care, Gran, won't you? 'Bye, then. Love."

I cradled the receiver, then lifted it again and got the number of the Lodge. It rang for a long time before a woman's breath-less voice answered it.

"Hullo? Strathbeg Lodge."

"Hullo. Is that Mrs Drew?"

"Speaking. Sorry to keep you waiting. I was out in the garden with the children. Who is it, please?"

"Oh, madam, it's Kate Herrick. Kathy Welland. I'm sorry to trouble you, but I was worried about my grandmother. She's just rung me up from the hospital, but she won't tell me much about it. I gathered it was some sort of gastric flu, but I did wonder if she was all right? Do you know about it?"

"Kathy, how nice to hear from you. Yes, your grandmother did have to go into the Cottage Hospital last week. She's been off colour for some time now, but she wouldn't admit to anything, so in the end Dr McLeod sent her in, really just for a rest, and he said while she was there they'd do some tests."

"Tests?" Somehow the word held a world of fearful speculation.

"Yes. These stomach upsets she's been having lately. Didn't she tell you? I think they were wondering about an ulcer. William, take that puppy out of here at once, *at once* — oh, hell, now see what's happened! Go and get a cloth. I don't know, ask Morag — no, do *not* ask Morag to do it, do it yourself. I'm so sorry, Kathy. I was saying. Your grandmother is coming home tomorrow, and I think we'll hear in a week or so if there's anything wrong. But really, she was just a bit tired and run down, with something like a mild flu, but Dr McLeod thought she should go in for examination. I don't honestly know any more, but if you'd like me to keep you in touch — you're coming up? Oh, great, that'll do her more good than anything else. Dear God, there's that puppy again. William! *William!* When will you get here, Kathy? Saturday night? I'll ask Angus to meet the train, shall I?"

"That's very kind of you, madam. Is her ladyship well?"

"Very well. We all are. I'll tell her you were asking. And do come and see us. Mother will be so pleased."

So it had been arranged. Angie had been kind, the train had run on time, Angus had met it with the pony-trap, and I had found Kirsty in capable charge at

Gran's cottage, with Gran herself in bed, and so relieved and happy to see me that she had gone almost straight to sleep. In the morning, with a visit from the district nurse and calls from two neighbours on their way home from the kirk, and Kirsty's busy presence, there had been no time for any private talk with Gran. The nurse, when I questioned her, was so professionally discreet that I was sure she knew nothing. Kirsty went back next door at lunch-time and I took Gran her soup and toast, but she looked tired, so when I went up to collect the dishes I smoothed the quilt over her, drew the curtains, and left her to sleep.

Then walked up the hill to sit in the sun and listen to the curlew's song.

3

Gran was sitting up against her pillows when I went upstairs after washing the supper dishes and saying goodnight to Kirsty, who had eaten with us.

"Well, and did you have a nice walk?"

"Lovely. How are you feeling now, Gran?"

"I'm fine. Now pull that chair up where I can see you properly. Hm. Very smart, I'm sure. Where'd you get that skirt, London? So they have tartans there now, do they?"

"England's pretty civilised these days. But you've had me worried, you know. What's it all about? If you say you're not really ill —"

"I'm not. I'll be up and about again in a wee while, but I can't say I'm not glad of a bit of a rest just now. It's a lot of standing, cooking, and my legs aren't as good as they were. Once this stomach's settled, I'll be as good as new, forbye a

bit of the rheumatism when the weather's
no' right." A trace of her girlhood accent
had come back, I noticed, to mix quite
kindly with the familiar North-country lilt.

"You want to go back to work? Truly?
You don't have to, you know."

"What would I do with myself if I didn't?
Nay, lass, we've had all this out and settled, so say no more. I'm as well here as
I'll ever be, with folk I know, and with you
coming home when you get your holidays,
and the family for ever in and out of the
door. It suits me fine, for all I miss Todhall
and the folks there. Now tell me about
yourself and this grand London job, for all
I'd have thought you should have something better than working in a shop."

It was plain that, whatever she had to
say to me, she would say it in her own
time, so I stifled my curiosity and told her
as much of my London news as I thought
would interest her. I had only seen her
once since my marriage, a flying visit in
the summer of 1945, as soon as term
ended, to tell her about Jon and that I
was giving up my school job and going,
at any rate until our affairs were sorted
out, to London. I had offered to stay with

her at Strathbeg, but, predictably, she would not hear of it. I must make a new life for myself now among my new friends (she meant, but did not say, "better myself") and try to let time heal the wounds of war. Not that she put it like that, but once again I knew what she meant; "stay where you're more likely to meet somebody else when you've got over it."

I knew she was hoping that this would be my news, but she bore very well with the daily doings at Platt's Plants, and then in her turn she brought me up to date with the happenings in the glen, and the affairs of the family at the House.

"I phoned them," I told her, "and Mrs Drew asked me to go over and see them."

"Well, of course you have to. Her ladyship's always asking after you. She'll tell you about it herself."

She was not looking at me as she spoke, but at something beyond the bedroom window. Not the blue hilltops of the summer evening; something further away even than they.

We had come to it at last. I said gently, "Tell me what?"

The roughened hands moved on the

quilt. "It was something I heard not long syne. Something the family are doing at Todhall."

"Yes? Do you mean them turning the Hall over into a hotel? I heard that, too; in fact, I think they've already started."

"Aye, they have. Annie Pascoe wrote me. Jim and Davey are working there." Jim Pascoe was the Todhall carpenter, and Davey was his son. His wife, "Aunty Annie" to me since childhood, was my godmother.

"Do you mind very much, Gran?"

"What's the use of minding?" Recovering herself, she was brisk. "It was a nice house, and I liked my kitchen — better than the one I've got here — but it had to come, and I'm well enough myself back here in the glen, and now with my own home. No, it's not the Hall, it's the house. Our own house. Rose Cottage."

"What about it? Do you mean they're altering that as well? Or are they selling it?"

"Not selling it, no, not yet. But there was talk of converting it — making one of those hotel places where folk fend for themselves, I forget what they call them."

"Annexes? Self-catering cottages?"

"That would be it. Like a hotel, but you do your own cooking. So if our cottage has to be made over, they'll be making big changes there, too."

"I suppose they'd have to, yes, surely. There'd have to be a better bathroom, and I dare say they'll put an electric cooker in, and a few other things, like a fridge and a washing-machine? But Granddad always said the building was sound, so they won't have to pull any of it down, will they?"

"That'd be enough, the electric stove, I mean. They'll be taking the fireplace out for it, or if they make the back-place into one of those wee kitchens — kitchenettes, they call them" — the word held a world of scorn — "they'll surely take out my old kitchen range and put a sitting-room fireplace into the front room."

"I suppose so. Gran, do you mind very much? I think — yes, I think I'll mind, a bit. And it was your home and Granddad's for all those years. You weren't hoping to go back one day, were you?"

She wasn't listening. A hand moved,

briefly, to touch my knee. "So that's it, Kathy. That's why I asked you to come."

"I don't see —"

"Listen. You never knew it, and nor, thank the good Lord, did your Aunt Betsy, but just aside the fireplace, on the left near the mantelshelf, there's a cupboard let into the wall."

"Is there? Really? I never saw one."

"No, you wouldn't, not without you knew where to look. Not to look, at that, but feel. It's tiny, no more than a tin box built into the wall, and it's been hidden — papered over — these many years. Do you mind the time we put that pretty paper on, with the autumn leaves and berries?"

"Not really. Was it — yes, wasn't it soon after Granddad died, just before Aunt Betsy came to stay? You and — you did it yourself, didn't you?"

"That's right. Lilias and I did it together." A silence, that I took care not to break. After a while she said, heavily, "For all that your Granddad was gone, that was a happy time."

I waited. When she spoke again she

was answering, I knew, what had not been said.

"And then Betsy came. She was a good woman, your great-aunt, make no mistake about that, for all she was never one to be easy with. Nor to share secrets with, neither. So she never knew about the cupboard."

"Gran, you said to the left of the fireplace. Do you mean behind the picture there?"

"I do. A holy text. Your aunt thought a lot of that text." A twinkle. "She was a tidy body about the house, your Aunt Betsy, and a good enough cook, but she was never great with the mop and duster. You might say that she dusted kind of reverent, without disturbing things, nor lifting them about, so she never noticed it. But I made sure. I only opened it up again the once, when she was from home, to put —" — a pause — "to put Lilias's bangle away. You'll remember that. They sent it over from Ireland after the accident. It was all there was, and I didn't want Betsy to see it, and maybe . . . Oh, well, never mind that. So then I made a real job of it, plastered it over nice and flat and matched the paper up, so if she ever did lift the picture down she'd not see anything, forbye a bit of a bubble in the pattern, where the keyhole is. Oh, it was safe enough, even at the spring-clean, or when we had to paper again. That's what your granddad used to call it, 'the safe'."

I said slowly: "I'm getting there, I think. There's something there still, in the 'safe'?"

"That's right. In all the clamjamphrie of the flitting, and giving the family a hand with their gear, I never thought about it. Nor at the time when your Aunt Betsy was took. The district nurse came most days, and Annie Pascoe helped out when I needed it, and what with one thing and another I never gave a thought to the safe. Maybe I was still thinking we'd be back there one day." A sigh, and another look through the window at something far away and long ago. Then back to me. "So what's there will still be there — that is, until they start pulling the fireplace out and find it."

"What is there, Gran?"

"Family things. Not valuable, except maybe for the five golden sovereigns that

Sir Giles, as was the Squire then, gave your Granddad on our wedding day, and which he'd never dream of spending, but all things I'd sorrow to lose. My ring that your Granddad gave me when we were promised, and the brooch my lady gave me for a wedding-present, lovely it was, you've seen it, pearls and those green stones, I misremember the name."

"Peridots."

"That's it. And there's your Mum's bracelet like I told you, and the letters your Granddad wrote me from France when he was fighting, if letters you can call them; one of them was written on a bit of cardboard torn off a box, and it got to me just as if it had been in a proper envelope, and registered at that. And his medals, he got two, and his watch and his wedding ring and a whole bundle of papers — my marriage lines, and your Mum's birth certificate and — well, all that sort of thing."

"My birth certificate, you mean?"

A silence.

"It's all right, Gran dear. I've seen it."

"You've seen it?" She was sharp. "How?"

"A copy, that's all. I wrote to Somerset

House for a copy. I wanted to see it for myself, and make sure. You see, I'd told Jon all about us — my family, I mean. I showed it to him. You do understand, don't you?"

"Aye," she said, "I do. And you did right." The clasped hands shifted on the coverlet. "Well, then, I don't need to tell you you'd get nothing from that. He's not on it."

"No." A pause, then I leaned forward to touch the old hands, lightly. "Gran."

"Eh, what now?"

"Look, Gran, I'm not sixteen any more and still at school. I've been married and widowed, and I'm twenty-four, and people think differently, anyway, since the war. I know you've always said you didn't know who he was, but if you're just trying to save me from hearing something I won't like —"

"Kathy love, don't. It's true I don't know. You have to believe me. She never told me. And guessing doesn't get you anywhere."

"Guessing? You can guess?"

My voice must have been sharp. She glanced up at me, then with a little gesture as if smoothing the air, said uncertainly: "It was nothing as anyone knew. Nothing to tell you."

"What was it? Gran, dear Gran, you must tell me, you really must. I've a right to know anything, anything at all."

"It's true, you have," she said, then, as if reluctantly, "all right. All I can tell you is what they said in the village at the time. There was gipsies camped in the lonnen — you remember Gipsy Lonnen?"

"Yes." It was a lane near Rose Cottage, a short cut to the station that the village rarely used.

"They were there that time, when she left. In the lonnen, with tents and a caravan. And they'd gone next day. So folks said she'd gone with them."

"They would. Maybe she did. But that doesn't mean it's anything to do with me, with who fathered me, I mean. I was six years old when she left."

"Yes. Well. The tale went that it was one of them, that she went with him some time when they'd been there before, and that when she left she went back to him. That's all. I told you it was nothing. Folks will say anything, and next time round they'll believe it." She touched my hand again. "I'm sorry, love. That's all there is. And now that she's gone, we'll never know."

Silence again. I stood up and went to the window. It was still light, the tranquil blue-grey twilight of the Highland summer. Somewhere a thrush was singing. I turned and spoke gently.

"Ah, well, it hardly matters now. I'm myself, and owing no one, except you and Granddad and Jon. Thanks for telling me, and let's forget it." I went back to the chair and sat down. "Okay, Gran. Now, have I got this right? You want me to go to Todhall and get your things from the safe before someone else finds them."

"That's it. But there's more."

"More?"

"Aye. Now I've got my own place here, I'd like fine to have the rest of my things sent up. The furniture, I mean, and some of the stuff that I left for your Aunt Betsy to use. Not all the furniture, I've neither room nor need for the beds and such, but there's my sideboard, and the good bits and pieces in Betsy's room, and some of the pictures and ornaments, and my rosebud tea-set, and his rocking-chair. I don't need the table, there's a good one here, and plenty chairs . . . I'll make a list. I've talked to her ladyship about it, and you're welcome to go there and take what you want. She's sent word that the men are to keep away till she tells them. So you'll go, won't you?"

"Well, of course I will. I'll go just as soon as you like."

"And keep a good eye on the movers, lass, there's not one of them I'd trust an inch not to break my rosebud china."

"I'll watch them, never fear."

"There's just one thing —"

"Yes?"

"The safe's locked," said Gran, looking guilty, "and I misremember where the key is."

I laughed. "That's useful. If I have to get one made to fit — is Bob Corner still at the smithy?"

"He is so, but whether he can turn his hand to anything as wee as that . . . Ah, well, I'll try to think on about the places I might have put the key, and you could look about. But it might take you a day or two."

"That's all right. Can I stay in the cottage, sleep there? I don't want to have to stay at the Black Bull and walk two miles each way."

"It's all right, you'll do fine at home. It's just as your Aunt Betsy had it, and your room's still as it was. Annie's been in to keep it aired and decent, but you'll be sure to air the mattress —"

I laughed. "Don't worry. I'll have the place liveable-in in no time. But what on earth is the village going to say when I arrive on my own out of the blue and open the cottage up?"

"It's that far from the village that they mayn't even notice. Not that I'd count on that while the Miss Popes are still there, nosy old bodies. And Miss Linsey, who's no better, and daft forbye. But" — a twinkle as she looked me up and down — "I'm wondering if they'll connect this smart young lady Mrs Herrick with little Kathy Welland that always had dirty knees and her hair in a fine tangle. If you keep yourself to yourself for a few days —"

"I'll do just that. And I didn't have dirty knees when I was sixteen, and going to the Sec! No, they'll know me all right, and they can think what they like. Now look how late it is. You ought to be asleep, and so should I. Would you like a hot drink or anything?"

"Seeing as I'm here on my native heath, as the saying is," said Gran, primly, "I'll take a wee dram, and you'll find the bottle at the back of the press there, where Kirsty won't find it without I see her."

"Okay. I'll get a glass. Two glasses, if I may?" I got to my feet. "And don't worry any more, Gran dear, I'll get your treasures safe for you, and anything else you want from home. You just think on, and we'll make a list in the morning."

4

I walked along to the House next morning.

I went, as I had always done, past the stables and the walled garden and into the yard behind the house, where a stout, middle-aged woman was pegging some tea-towels out on the line. This must be Morag; Gran had told me that the only other "help" now was a girl of sixteen who came mornings, and I could hear the vacuum cleaner going somewhere behind an upstairs window.

Morag, who was new since my last visit to Strathbeg, did not look in the least like the apprentice that Gran had described to me; she was well into her forties, looked immensely capable, and I thought I would have backed her clootie dumplings against anyone else's *haute cuisine* anywhere.

She turned as I approached.

"Good morning," I said. "I'm Mrs Welland's granddaughter Kathy. You must be Morag? I'm sorry, but I don't know your other name. It's Mrs —?"

"Morag'll do fine. So you're Kathy." We shook hands. She looked me up and down, not rudely, but with a sort of cautious appraisal. "You're welcome, I'm sure. Her ladyship said you might be coming down."

"Is it convenient now?" I really just called to see — I could come later, but I may be going south again tomorrow."

"It's all right, come away in. You might as well come this way now you're here. It's through the kitchen."

"I know. It's the way I'm used to."

She gave me another look where I thought I saw a touch of sour approval. "Aye, well . . . And how's your grandma?"

"Glad to be home again. Hospitals are good places to get out of. You know, this feels a bit like home to me, too. The kitchen looks just the same, and you've been baking . . . It smells good."

A tightening of the lips that might be meant for a smile. "Scones. I'd a mind to send some up to Mrs Welland, but she'd maybe no' think they were good enough."

"She'd like it fine, I'm sure, and I'd certainly appreciate them, if you'd let me take them up. Thanks very much." I tried a touch of diplomacy. "It's nice that she can be so easy in her mind, with you here. Do you come from somewhere in the glen?"

"No. I'm from Inverness, but I like it fine here in the summer. The winter's another thing, but there's a while to go yet before that. Well, if you'll bide a bit while I see to the oven . . ." She lifted the baking-sheet out and began to set the delicious-smelling scones out on the rack to cool.

"The house is very quiet, isn't it?" I said. "Where are the children? I'd have liked to see them. William wasn't much more than a baby when I was here before, and Sarah was in her pram. Are they out?"

It seemed that they were. "Himself", as she called Sir James, was down by the river after the fish, and the Major was along with him. Mrs Drew had gone up to the village to meet the Bank — I would mind, said Morag, setting the last scone in place, that Monday was the day the Bank came to the glen — but her ladyship was in her room writing letters. I'd mind the room? The wee sitting-room by the side door? I did? Then did I want to go through now, or would she tell her lady-ship I was here?"

I hesitated. "Would you mind telling her, Morag? I don't like just to walk through if she's busy."

That nod of approval again. She wiped her hands on her apron, took it off, then led me along the well-known passage to the green baize door, that traditional bar-rier between the back and the front of the house. I could not guess what Morag had heard about me, nor what she had ex-pected, but it was obvious that, in her view, I had quite properly kept to my own side of that barrier.

Going through the green door was like going back in time. It was all just as I remembered it. There was the wide hall, carpeted with worn and faded rugs which had once been valuable, and cluttered, rather than furnished, with enormous cup-boards and chests rather in need of pol-ishing, and a long table littered with gloves and newspapers and copies of the *Scottish Field* and a gardener's trug of hand-tools. Against the once-crimson walls hung pictures in heavy gilt frames, painted it seemed mainly in shades of sepia and Vandyke brown. All familiar; I had dusted or polished every item. Familiar, too, was the big bowl, full of water for the dogs, that stood on the floor by the drawing-room door. I had refilled it scores of times, carrying it carefully from the cloakroom by the front door. But never, I thought, as carefully as I would carry it now that I could recognise it for what it was, an immensely valuable piece of blue-and-white Ming. Beside it lay a half-chewed bone, presumably left there by William's puppy.

The sitting-room door was ajar, and Morag pushed it open to let a shaft of sunshine through onto these dim splendours.

"It's Kathy Welland, m'lady."

Lady Brandon turned and laid down her pen, then got up from her writing-table and came, smiling, to meet me.

"Oh, Kathy, good morning. Thank you, Morag. Kathy, how nice to see you, and how well you're looking. Come in. What a lovely day, isn't it? Sit down, my dear, and tell me how your grandmother is."

For all the years that had passed, and all that had happened in them of change, both in myself and in the world at large, I felt awkward as I went forward to shake hands. Last time I had been in that sunny little room it was to clean out the fire and do the dusting. But Lady Brandon, easy and kind as always, and of course vastly experienced, saw us both smoothly through the moment, and soon had me settled with her in the sunshine of the bay window, answering her questions.

She was a slightly built woman, too thin for her height, but with the elegance that this gave her. I noticed with wry amusement that she was dressed very much as I was, silk blouse, tweed skirt, woollen jacket. Uniform, almost, this side of the baize door. It didn't stop me feeling tongue-tied, and wanting to sit on the edge of my chair, but as she talked on, charmingly, about Gran, I found myself relaxing into naturalness and even ease.

"I'm hoping to call and see her soon," she said. "Perhaps this afternoon? Do you think she's up to it?"

"I'm sure she'd love to see you, my lady. She looks a bit thinner than I remember, and for once she admits to feeling tired, but she keeps saying there's nothing much wrong with her, except what the flu left behind." I hesitated. "I can't help wondering — this talk about tests at the hospital. She won't say anything to me, but I did wonder, do you know anything about it, I mean, if there might be something serious?"

"I'm afraid I don't know anything about that, but I do know that Dr McLeod isn't worried about her."

"He said so?"

"Yes. So I think you needn't be too anxious. I don't think your grandmother will be an invalid for very long. Were you planning to stay and look after her? I'm sure she'll love having you here. How long can you stay?"

"I've got a fortnight due to me, though I could take longer if I needed it. But actually I'm going south almost straight away. You see" — at her look of surprise — "it's Rose Cottage. Because of the plans to alter it, I mean. She's a bit anxious to get the rest of her things sent up, now that she's got a place of her own here. She wants me to go down straight away to see to it."

"I see. But is there any hurry about it? They won't do anything at the cottage until we give them the All Clear. I promised her that."

"Yes, I know. But — well, there's something she's worried about, and she wants me to see about it, and I think that — I mean, if her mind was at rest —" I faltered into silence. I did not think I could explain about Gran's "treasures" lying forgotten in their hiding-place.

I need not have worried that she would pursue it. She said quickly, "It's all right, my dear. It's your grandmother's affair, she must do as she wants. Of course she would like her own things about her, and it's good that she has you to see to the move for her. Moving house, even only half a house, is a frightful job."

"It is only half a house, anyway — less than half what's there, I think. We made a list, and I've brought it for you to see, because she says she can't remember just what was already there — belonging to the Hall, I mean, when they moved in. Things like the big press in the back kitchen, and the table and chairs — she's leaving those anyway — and, well, here's the list. That's as much as she can remember of what's hers. If you would look at it, please, my lady, and see if it's right?"

"I'm sure it is. There's no need — very well, as you've gone to the trouble. Let me see it."

She took the paper. A brief silence as she studied, or pretended to study, the list we had made, and I looked around me at the familiar room. Pretty, washed-out chintzes and a Chinese carpet. A big bowl of flowers on a stand, and more in a vase on the mantelpiece, beside an assortment of fragile-looking china that I remembered all too well. Photographs everywhere, in silver frames. There were various ones of the children at different stages of growth, and of their mother, Mrs Drew, as a girl, as a debutante, and then as a bride. Beside her, on the bureau, was one of her brother, the dead son, Gilbert, young and smiling, in uniform, dark-haired and dark-eyed. Like me. Like an older brother. And indeed, he had been the nearest I had ever had to a brother; he had sometimes come down to the gardens when I had been there with Granddad, and I had been allowed to follow and admire him as his own sister never would — to retrieve the ball when he practised his bowling at the makeshift nets, to watch when he climbed the big cedar by the tennis court, to wait with the net while he fished the beck beside Rose Cottage . . .

I tore my eyes from the photograph and my mind away from what I was thinking. Had thought before; had tried not to think. Lady Brandon was folding the paper and she handed it back to me. "Well, please thank your grandmother for letting me see this, Kathy. I'm sure it's absolutely right. To tell you the truth I've quite forgotten what's there, and I don't know if an inventory was ever made, but please tell her that she's welcome to anything she wants to take."

"And it's all right for me to stay there while I'm seeing about the moving?"

She assured me that it was, and I thanked her, and said how much Gran appreciated having her own place here in Strathbeg, and how well she seemed to get along with Kirsty, and then for some minutes more we talked about the new plans for Tod Hall, and what might happen to Rose Cottage. I gathered that nothing had been settled there; the cottage might simply be re-let, if there was a ready taker, or even sold, "always providing that your grandmother doesn't want to go back there. I know how one feels about a place that has been home for so many years."

I thought that there was some personal feeling there for her, but said nothing.

She smiled at me, as if reading my thoughts, and added: "I don't know if your grandmother knows, but we're not leaving the place entirely. I've persuaded my husband to keep part of the south wing, the bit that overlooks the rose garden, and we're having a kitchen put in there — you remember the old flower-room? The joiners are working on that now. The main conversion is to be done by a big contractor, of course, but we did want to give our part of the work to local people, and the Pascoes always do such a good job."

"I'm sure the village will be pleased you're still there." I said. "The Hall will be missed, I know."

"I have such memories," she said.

There was a short silence, and I wondered if I should go, but then she smiled at me again, and said, gently: "I haven't said, Kathy, how very sorry I was — we all were — to hear of your loss. It has been hard for you, I know." I made some sort of response, and then she asked me about my work in London, and whether I planned to go back to teaching, and the conversation slipped easily back to everyday things.

She went on to offer me coffee, but this I declined, more to save Morag's feelings than for any other reason. So I merely thanked her, took my leave, and went back through the green baize door to have coffee and newly baked scones in the kitchen with Morag.

5

At seven minutes to three on a warm June afternoon the train from Sunderland rattled into Todhall station and stopped with a jerk and a long, sighing puff of steam. On the platform was a porter I didn't recognise, a youth of perhaps sixteen, who would have been a small boy when I was last at home, but the old station-master just emerging from his office, watch in hand, was Mr Harbottle, who had been there for as long as I could remember. He did not see me, being busy consulting his watch, and nodding over it with satisfaction. The two-fifty-three was, as usual, exactly on time.

"Toddle!" shouted the porter, though no one but myself was alighting in the sleepy afternoon, then, "Toddle, miss?" as he opened the carriage door for me, and reached a hand out to take my case.

Coupled with his engaging grin and outstretched hand, it made a tempting invitation, but I controlled myself, saying merely, "Yes. Thank you," and stepped down to the platform. I handed him my ticket, and turned to speak to Mr Harbottle, but he was already on his way along the platform with his green flag at the ready, to exchange some no doubt vital information with the engine-driver whom he only saw four times a day and would not see again until five-fourteen, when the Earl Grey (as the stubby black and green engine was rather grandly named) pulled its coaches back to Sunderland.

Mr Harbottle looked at his watch again, the flag was lifted, the engine blew another noisy cloud of steam, the couplings clanged and strained, and the train chugged off. Without another glance in my direction, Mr Harbottle put his watch away, picked up a spade which was leaning against a pile of sleepers, and went back to what he had presumably been doing before the train came in — digging his new potatoes up and sorting them lovingly into an empty fire-bucket.

So much for Kathy Welland's homecoming. At my elbow the porter said, rather anxiously: "It's all of two mile into the village, miss. No bus nor nothing. Didn't they tell you when you booked?"

"It's all right. I haven't much to carry. I don't need the big case straight away. Can you keep it here till I can send for it? I can manage the other one easily." I had brought a light holdall with what I needed for the night.

"Easy. It can stay in the office." He swung it up and I followed him along the platform, past the chocolate machine (it was empty; I wondered if it had ever been refilled after Prissy and I took the last piece out six years ago), and the penny-in-the-slot Try-Your-Weight machine, and the flourishing beds of geraniums and calceolarias and love-in-a-mist.

"You staying in the village, miss? If it's the Black Bull, they're sending a cart along to meet the eight-sixteen in the morning. They've got beer coming then. I could put your bag on it if you like?"

The Black Bull was the village's single pub, four doors up from the vicarage, and next door to Barlow's shop where Prissy and I had spent our halfpennies on liquorice bootlaces and gobstoppers. The pub's loaded cart, I knew, would not want to turn aside down the steep lane that led from the high road to Rose Cottage.

"No, not the Black Bull," I said, "but don't you worry, I can get it picked up tomorrow. Thanks all the same." I gave him sixpence, which was twice the normal tip, but worth it for that smile again, as, with a cheerful "Ta, miss," he carried my case through the door marked "Station Master" and flanked by tubs of geraniums and lobelias.

As I went out into the sunny roadway I saw Mr Harbottle, still busy with his spade, getting on with his day's work at the far end of the platform. No doubt he was preparing, as he had done every year since long before I was born, to scoop most of the Firsts at the local Agricultural Show in July. Meanwhile Todhall would come, as usual, high on the Commended list for the county's best-kept station . . .

Memory Lane. Well, I still had two long, hot miles of it to go, if I went by the road, but I knew all the bypaths and short cuts for miles around, and had come comfortably dressed for the walk. I followed the road for perhaps a quarter of a mile, till I reached a field gate giving on a track that showed the triple ruts of the farmer's horse and cart. The track, shaded by an over-grown hedgerow, led along the side of a hayfield almost overdue for cutting, and deep in flowering grasses. A couple of hundred yards further, and I came to a gap in the hedgerow which had been roughly blocked by a criss-cross of hazel stems.

It was no more than a token barrier, easy to step over. I stepped over, and picked my way carefully down a steep bank into what had once been a lane, but was now little more than a path be-tween high banks overgrown with ferns and weeds, and overshadowed by the rampant hedges. It was a deep, secret place. Gipsy Lonnen, the gipsies' lane.

It had changed, with time. Years ago it had been an open, grass-grown lane where sometimes the travelling gipsies would pitch for a few nights, nights when we, the village children, were strictly for-bidden to venture out after sunset. We had obeyed, frightened into obedience with tales of children stolen away by the gipsies, tales which somehow got mixed up in my childish mind with the legendary abductions of Kilmeny and the little changeling boy and other creatures of poetry and fairy-tale.

Even by day, when no gipsies camped there, the lonnen had been a scary place. At some time in the past a caravan had been abandoned there. A frightened horse, possibly, had backed it sharply into the bank, and a wheel had broken adrift, and the shafts with it. The wreck, abandoned, had rotted and fallen still further apart, but it retained the shape of the caravan, and to our childish minds it was a place where the wicked gipsy ghosts of fiction lurked, ready to pounce. The boys, when we girls were watching, would dare one another to run up the lonnen and touch the shafts or the steps of the van, but only the hardiest spirits ever did this. The rest of us, cowards all, thought ourselves brave enough if we climbed down through the gap with the hazel-boughs and then ran hard along the half-mile of stony grass to the stile and the field above Rose Cottage. The only time that Gipsy Lonnen lost its terror for us was in bramble-time, when adults and children together took their baskets and buckets into the lane to harvest the blackberries.

Now I was an adult myself, and it was midafternoon, and there was no sign of gipsies. And the lonnen saved almost a mile. Somewhere out of sight to my right, presumably hidden now under the over-growth of bramble and sapling, lay the remains of the gipsy van. I turned the other way. There was still a narrow path reasonably clear between high banks em-broidered with wild roses and the white bramble-flowers. Campion and ragged robin showed everywhere among the crowding ferns and Jack-by-the-hedge, and the air was filled with the fresh, lovely smell of wild garlic, late-flowering in the shade.

The sense of smell is the hair-trigger of memory. I walked through the scented half-dusk full of garlic and fern and briar, trying not to think too much about what Gran had told me of the village gossip. Lilias and a gipsy? My young mother run-ning off that night, with her Gladstone bag in her hand and tears on her face, to some vagrants' camp in the lane? At least, I thought, I need not be haunted by the broken caravan; that could have had nothing to do with her. It had been there as long as I could remember. Or had it? I had been six when she went. Had our childhood games gone as far back as that? Or was that the haven she had run to that night? Whose had it been?

I managed to thrust the thoughts out of mind, and walked on. Another half-mile along that nostalgically scented lane, then came the next gap in the bank, and the stile. I climbed over, back into sunshine and a freshly moving breeze, and the open, sloping field where, as children, we had come Every Easter-time to roll our hard-boiled eggs in a sort of version of the conkers game played in autumn with horse-chestnuts. At the foot of the Pace-Egg Field, as we had called it, was another stile. This, too, led into a lane, but an open sunny lane that sloped gently down towards a stream crossed by a wooden foot-bridge.

And a few yards upstream from the bridge, snugly set in what had once been a lovingly tended garden, was Rose Cottage.

I remember, I remember
The house where I was born,
The little window where the sun
Came peeping in at morn . . .

I believe that anyone returning to their childhood's home is surprised to find how small it is. It was only seven years since I had lived there, but even so, Rose Cottage had shrunk. It was tiny, a genuine cottage, two-and-a-half up and two down, with a "back place" built out behind, over which a diminutive bathroom had been added. The two-and-half up had dormer windows projecting from the thatch, and the little window of what had been my bedroom had not allowed the morning sun very much of a peep. The garden showed every evidence of the past years' neglect, in a joyous riot of overgrown rose-bushes and weeds and summer flowers, but someone — presumably one of the Pascoes — had cleared the front path, and the windows and curtains looked fresh and clean.

I dumped my holdall in the porch, inserted Gran's key into the lock, and pushed the front door open.

It opened straight into the living-room, the kitchen as we had always called it. This was a smallish room, some twelve feet square, with an open grate flanked by metal trivets, with the oven alongside. Inside the high fender the hearth had been freshly holystoned, and Gran's old plate-warmer still stood there, a curious affair of turned wood, like a giant caltrop. All was just as I remembered it, the hearthrug made of hooked rags, warm and bright, with Granddad's rocking-chair to one side, and a rather less comfortable chair opposite; the solidly made table, which, scrubbed daily till the grain of the wood stood up like ribbing, was used for everything, baking, ironing, eating from, but which between jobs was covered with a red chenille cloth bordered with bobbles. The sideboard, backed by an ornate mirror, was covered with a long runner edged with crocheted lace, on which stood a pair of vases, much admired by me as a child, with a design of richly sprawling roses and forget-me-nots. Between the vases stood a rather lovely old oil-lamp, set aside as an ornament after "the electric" came to the village in the twenties. Above the sideboard hung a framed text, THOU, GOD, SEEST ME, and a flight of china ducks soared on a slant up the wall.

All this I took in at a glance, also that the place was as tidy, as newly dusted, as if it was still lived in. Mrs Pascoe, whose work, of course, this must be, had also been kind enough to leave a bottle of milk and a loaf on the table, with the bonus of a poke of tea and a note which said, "Welcome home and I've told the milk. Bottle in bed. Be down later. A. P."

No difficulty in interpreting this very real welcome-home, but I made no immediate move to fill the kettle or unpack any of the stand-by provisions I had brought. I would have been less than human if my eyes had not gone straight to the wall at the left of the fireplace.

Another text hung there, one that had been infinitely more inhibiting to a small, highly imaginative child. It said, in large capitals: CHRIST IS THE UNSEEN GUEST AT EVERY MEAL: THE SILENT LISTENER TO EVERY CONVERSATION. I remembered my own childish surprise that Aunt Betsy had dared to speak as she did sometimes with the Unseen Guest sitting right there and taking in every word.

I lifted the text down.

"You can't see it," Gran had said. "It's tiny, no more than a tin box built into the wall, and it's papered over."

It wasn't papered over. Someone had cut cleanly along the edges of the door, removing both plaster and paper, and there, stark against the small pink roses and faded grey trellis of the wallpaper, was Gran's safe, just a small metal box cemented into the brickwork, with a key-hole showing, but no key.

I must have stood there for some minutes, staring blankly, before it occurred to me to try to open the metal door. I did not waste time looking for the key, which, as Gran had told me after much thought, might be in any of the drawers or vases or other hiding-places in the kitchen or anywhere else. I found a table-knife and inserted it, with some difficulty, into the crack by the lock, and tried levering the door open. It would not budge.

So, it was still locked. In some relief I stood back. Perhaps after all the safe hadn't been broken into: it must be quite a few years since this paper had been pasted on, and it was possible that Gran herself had cut it back to put some later treasure into hiding, and then had forgotten about it, as she had forgotten the whereabouts of the key.

The key. I peered into the vases on the sideboard. The first one appeared to hold nothing but two hairpins, a halfpenny, and a dead moth. The other was a quarter full of papers, and the assorted small rubbish of years. Well, later would have to do. No point in starting to worry tonight. I hung the text back in its place, and — the first really important action of every homecoming — went and put the kettle on.

6

I finished my tea, put away the iron ration of food that I had brought to last me till morning, then, spreading a sheet of newspaper on the table, I tipped out the contents of the second vase.

A clutter of papers, a couple of clothes-pegs, a toffee rather past its best, three safety pins and a thimble, and that was all. No key.

The sideboard drawers next, with the same result. No key.

I looked around me. The table drawer. The big cupboard in the alcove to the right of the fireplace. Two more vases on the mantelpiece, and a hundred other places where a tiny key might lie hidden. And then there were the back premises and the bedrooms.

It would have to wait. I had, in any case, a strong suspicion that Gran had taken the key with her to Strathbeg, and forgotten all about it. It was just the sort of thing she would have tucked away in some pocket of the enormous holdall she called her handbag, that held everything from her purse and essential papers like ration-book and identity card, along with her pills and her spectacles and her knitting and her prayer book, and other necessities of her life.

I picked up my own holdall and opened the door in the wall opposite the fireplace, which gave on the steep, enclosed staircase. My steps rapped, echoing, on bare boards. At the top was a small landing where Gran's beloved clock stood; a miniature long-case, the kind they called a grandmother clock. I remembered its gentle chime punctuating the long days of childhood. I would set it going, I thought, before I went to bed.

My room had certainly shrunk. Two steps from the door to the foot of the iron bedstead that stood against one wall. Three from the bedside to the window sunk in the alcove under the slope of the ceiling. It was hard to believe that I had shared it with my mother. It had been her room until Aunt Betsy came to stay, after which I had moved in with her, while Gran, giving Aunt Betsy the larger of the two front rooms, had taken over my little room at the back.

I dumped the bag and went to the window. I had to stoop to see out. There was a stool in the alcove, and I knelt on that and pushed the window open to look out.

Beyond the weedy garden with its riot of rose-bushes, nothing had changed. The beck, wide here and quiet, slid past below the bridge. Willows and wild roses, cuckoo-pint and king-cups, and a wood-pigeon crooning in the elms.

And someone crossing the bridge to approach the garden gate.

It was someone I knew well, my god-mother Mrs Pascoe, who had been my mother's friend and had "helped out" at the Hall when there were guests to stay. She was a little older than Lilias would have been, somewhere nearing her fifties, I guessed; a capable, comfortable woman who never seemed to be either fussed or short-tempered — a valuable quality in the sometimes stressful world of a crowded kitchen.

I went downstairs and opened the door to her.

"Aunty Annie! How lovely to see you!" We embraced warmly. "Do come in! And thank you for the welcome home. I had tea straight away, thanks to you, but the kettle won't take long to boil up again if you'd like a cup —"

"No, dearie, no. I'll be going home soon. I just came over to see if you'd got here. I thought you might be on that train. Well" — following me into the kitchen — "let's have a look at you. You look well, Kathy. You've changed a bit, but then how many years is it? Six? Seven?"

"Nearly seven, I'm afraid, but you haven't changed at all! Not a day older! How's Uncle Jim? And Davey?" Davey was their son, who worked alongside his father. He was about my age, and had been in my class at the village school, and later at the Sec.

"Oh, they're all right. Nothing ever ails them. But what about your Gran? She didn't sound so clever when she phoned me."

"I'm afraid she's had a bad time, flu and then some gastric trouble. They took her into hospital for treatment and tests, but we hadn't heard the result when I came south. Did she phone you from the hospital? Well, she's home now, but she's keeping her bed for a bit. Look, won't you sit down?"

"Well, thanks, but just for a minute. I only came along to see if you had all you need."

"I'm fine, thanks. I brought enough for tonight, and I'll go up to the village tomorrow. Thank you for the milk and the tea — Gran did tell me that you were coming in to fix the place up, but it was just wonderful to get here and find everything so lovely. You wouldn't know we'd ever been away! I hope it wasn't too dirty."

"It wasn't so bad. I've been coming down about once a month to open up and stop the place getting damp, so there wasn't all that to do, bar a few spiders to chase out, and a fall of plaster over by the fireplace there. But nothing to worry about, and you can see there's no damage to the ceiling."

I looked where she pointed, but it wasn't the ceiling I was thinking about. I was remembering the plasterless state of the square of wall behind the Unseen Guest. Presumably she hadn't lifted the

picture down to see that. And possibly —
a less comfortable thought — the plaster
had been chipped away during the last
three or four weeks, since she had last
been in to air the cottage . . .

"How long d'you reckon you'll want to
stay?" she was asking.

"What? Sorry. Oh, not long, just enough
to get Gran's things sorted and the ones
she wants packed up. I suppose you
knew that she'd decided to stay up at
Strathbeg? I doubt if she'll ever come
back here."

"She didn't say much, but I thought that
would be how it was. I suppose she feels
at home there. Oh, well. Look, dearie, can
I change my mind? I'll take a cup, if you'll
have another with me yourself?"

Over the fresh brew of tea I told her
about Gran's new house in Strathbeg, and
the furniture that was to be sent north.
She already knew something about it from
Gran herself, and had talked it over with
her husband. Mr Pascoe knew a good
firm of carriers in Sunderland who would
do the moving, she said, and she and
Davey, when he could, would help me
with the packing.

"They're working at the Hall now, aren't they? Lady Brandon told me the family were keeping some rooms for themselves."

"That's so. It'll be a nice place for them when it's done, and it'll be good to see them back here again. Todhall isn't the same without the family. The word goes that Sir James isn't likely to come back much, but my lady always loved this place, and I dare say Miss Margery'll be here with the children."

"Have you heard anything about the plans for Rose Cottage?"

But she had not. A firm of contractors from Darlington were being called in to do the main work of the hotel conversion, but the Brandons had made it a condition that local tradesmen should be employed there, too, whenever possible.

"Stands to reason," said Mrs Pascoe, "that there's nobody knows more about that old house and its fixings than my Jim, and when it comes to the plumbing you can't get better than Peter Brigstock." She set down her cup. "Now, how about you? I should have said sooner, I was sorry about your trouble, we all were. An airman, wasn't he, your husband?"

"Yes. Bombers. He'd nearly finished his tour, only another four missions to go. Ah, well, that's the way it went. It seems a long time ago now. We didn't have very long, but we were happy while it lasted."

"It was a terrible thing. We were that sorry when we heard. But your Gran said he left you all right — comfortable, I mean? Well, that's a bit to the good. And you're living in London now, with a good job?"

"Well, it's a job. A friend offered it to me, and it's pleasant work, in a big plant nursery. Not very well paid, but I enjoy it, and luckily that's all that matters."

"You didn't go back to teaching, then?"

"No. I didn't want to, but I had to do something." I didn't elaborate. I had never wanted to admit, even to myself, what a vacuum Jon's death had left in my life. With marriage had come a feeling of belonging, plans for the future, a sense of identity, of being. The satisfying, perhaps, of something primitive in every woman; the need for a warm cave-place of her own, and the family round the fire. Quite apart from the grief of it, his death had pushed me, so to speak, back on the world again, with my own solitary way to make, and not much idea of which way to go.

I put the thought aside, and asked about the people in Todhall that I remembered.

"Will I find the place much changed?"

"Not really. The village was lucky in the war. Your Gran would tell you about it, I don't doubt."

"She told me Arthur Barton lost an arm, and about Sid Telfer being killed. How's Mrs Telfer making out? There were three children, weren't there?"

"There were. And there are five now, so the less said about her the better." She must have remembered then that she was talking to another child of shame, because she pushed the empty cup back rather hastily and got to her feet.

"I'd best be getting along. I had a word with Ted Blaney yesterday — you remember the Blaneys at Swords Farm? — and he'll stop by with milk tomorrow. If you have a word with him he'll bring what you need from the village."

"Or give me a lift in? He always used to."

"I dare say he might still," she said, and suddenly smiled. "If you change to something a bit less London. His cart's usually half full of straw, or even a hen or two in a crate. Not but what you look very nice, at that. So, I'll be getting back to the Hall. I go up there most days while the men's working. It's just Jim and Davey there now, and you'd be welcome if you want to come by and see what's going on."

"I'd like to, very much. Thank you."

I went to the front gate with her, and stood while she made her way back across the bridge. There was a sort of secondary driveway there, which led up through the woods that edged the park and then past the walled garden and into the back quarters of the Hall. It was the way my grandfather had walked daily to his work, and where I, as a small child, had so many times gone with him.

I turned back into the cottage, hesitated for a moment by the hidden safe, then, shrugging, left it for tomorrow, and went up to my bedroom to unpack.

7

Try as I would, I could not set aside my curiosity about Gran's safe. As soon as I had unpacked my few things, and refilled the hot-water-bottle in the freshly made-up bed, I went out to the toolshed which stood under the lilac tree behind the cottage.

The toolshed had always been my grandfather's special place. It was small, a wooden hut with a window in one side, under which stood a sturdy bench, and on the other wall a row of six-inch nails from which hung his garden tools. If he had needed any special implement, he borrowed it from the big collection up at the Hall; here he kept only the basics, spade, fork, hoe, rake, shears, and in a wall-rack beside the window, the hand-tools such as trowels and secateurs. A metal tool-box under the bench held chisels and screwdrivers and boxes of nails and so forth. The barrow was kept outside under a lean-to. There was no lawn-mower; we had no lawn.

The shed had always been kept tidy, but when I saw it that day it was tidy indeed. It was empty. All the tools had gone, including the tool-box. I checked the door, which had been locked, and which I had opened with the key that hung in the back kitchen. No sign there of tampering or damage. I looked outside; the barrow was there. But all that could be carried away had gone.

It was possible, of course, that Gran had got rid of the things, sold them or given them away when she went north. It didn't concern me much, except that I would need something rather stronger than a kitchen knife to tackle the door of her safe. Feeling suddenly impatient, I glanced at my watch. Half past five. I would walk up to the Hall and borrow the tools I needed. If there were still gardeners employed there, they would have gone off at five, and the gate into the walled garden would probably be locked, but I knew where the key was kept. I got my jacket from the cottage, and set out for the Hall.

Across the bridge, up through the belt

of woodland that edged the park, and then a short cut through a landscaped glade to the high wall of the vegetable garden and the archway with the beautiful iron gate that had been made, nearly a hundred years ago, in the smithy next door to the vicarage.

I did not need, after all, to feel up behind the Virginia creeper for the key. Just before I reached it the gate opened, and a young man came out, wheeling a bicycle. A workman, by his clothes, and what my grandfather would have called "a well-set-up young feller". He looked to be about my age, a capable-looking young man with brown hair and grey eyes, where I thought I could still see the quiet, clever seventeen-year-old who had been in my class at school.

He checked when he saw me. "Were you looking for someone? I'm the last. Everyone knocked off at five."

"I — it's Davey, isn't it? It *is* Davey?"

"Aye, but — ? Hang on a minute. You're Kathy, Kathy Welland. Mum said you were here. We-ell!" The last syllable was drawn out with a world of meaning as he looked me over from head to foot.

"Wouldn't you have known me?" I heard, in my own voice, a kind of wistfulness. Here in the place where as a child I had spent so many hours with my grandfather, where I had learned so much of what I needed to carry into the world, and where I had sometimes played with this very boy when his father had been working at the Hall, something in me was responding strongly to the scents and sights of a happy childhood, and Davey, standing there so changed, and looking at me with a mixture of friendly surprise and reserve, was part of it.

I could hear, too, that my voice had taken back, as a kind of echo, some of the country sounds it had rejected. Kate Herrick or Kathy Welland? Which was I? Which did I want to be?

"Sure I'd have known you," he said. "The sun was right behind you there, and you spoke different, but now I see you, yes, I'd know you anywhere." He gave a nod. "Good to see you back, Kathy. You okay at the cottage?"

"Fine, thank you. Were you going that way?"

"Yes. I'm going to the station to pick up

a package for my Dad. I'll walk down with you if you like. Were you wanting something up here, or were you just out for a walk? Mum said you might come up some time, but she went home when Dad left with the van."

"I really came up to see if I could borrow a hammer and chisel. All the tools have gone from our shed. If you'll wait a minute while I get them —"

"No need to bother going in there. I've got my tools with me. I can lend you what you want. What's it for? Mum didn't say anything needed doing." I saw then that a satchel of tools was strapped behind the bicycle. As he spoke he busied himself pulling the flap open, then turned with a chisel in his hand. "This do? What d'you want it for? I'll come in if you like and fettle it for you."

I took it from him. "Well, thank you, but —" I stopped. The chisel looked familiar, and yes, there on the handle, burned into the wood, were the initials H.W.

I looked up to see Davey grinning. It made him look years younger, and very like the boy I had known before time and the war years had taken and changed us both.

He gave a nod. "Yes, that's where they all went. You might've guessed. Your Gran told me to take the lot, 'and see you make good use of them, my lad,' she said, you know the way she talks. But you're welcome to any of them if you need them. Goes without saying."

"No, no. Just for the one job, and —" I made a decision. "And yes, Davey, I would be glad if you'd help me. If you've time, that is; I don't know how long it may take. I'll tell you about it on the way down."

We went together, Davey wheeling his bicycle, and as we went I told him about the safe, and something of what Gran had said. "There are things like Granddad's watch and medals, and some jewellery of Gran's, and some family papers. I never even knew about it, and I honestly believe she'd forgotten all about it herself till she heard that they might be going to alter the cottage."

"We'll get them out, no bother. But wasn't there a key?"

"Yes, but of course she's forgotten where

she hid it. That's the other thing.I had a look at the safe, Davey, and the plaster's been cut away from the door. Someone's been there, but whether the door's been opened or not I can't tell. If it has, then it's been opened with the key. There's no sign of forcing."

"Hm. Sounds queer to me. No wonder you're in a hurry to take a look at it." A frowning pause. "I suppose your Gran couldn't have been at it herself some time back, and forgotten that as well?"

"I thought of that. But your mother told me just now that there was a trace of plaster on the floor there when she was cleaning, and that must have been pretty recent."

"It's loose stuff. Even if the wall was broken some time back, the plaster might still be flaking. Don't you worry yourself about it, we'll soon see. I suppose you did look for the key?"

"Yes. I've not had time yet for a real search, though I've looked in the obvious places, but it must be very small — the keyhole's tiny — and it could be any-where, so I thought I might as well try and lever the door open somehow, just to set my mind at rest. Break it open, even. Gran's not likely to be using the place again."

We had reached the bridge. He paused with the bicycle hoisted half up the steps. "So it's true what Mum said? You're leaving Todhall for good?"

"Yes. Gran seems to want to stay at Strathbeg, and I've got a job in London now that I like, though if it came to that I'd be quite happy to give it up and go north to look after her. Anyway, they're selling our cottage, or making it over or something, aren't they?"

"Nobody seems rightly to know what's to be done with it. In any case" — he heaved his bicycle up over the steps and wheeled it across the bridge — "busting your Gran's safe open won't hardly matter. Or if you like I can ask my Dad? It sounds to me as if he, or my Grandpa even, must have put that hidey-hole in, and there maybe another key. But if you're in a hurry," he added, cheerfully, as he propped the bicycle beside the cottage gate, "we can break it open now. Soon see, when I've had a look at it."

"What time do you have to be at the station?"

"Doesn't matter. The package'll be left in the office, and there'll be someone there till the last train." He followed me into the cottage, dumping his tool-bag on the table, and watched while I lifted down the Unseen Guest.

"Hm, yes." He looked thoughtfully at the cleared piece of wall, and the metal square framed by paper and broken plaster. "And my Mum said there'd been a fall of plaster here?"

"Yes. Davey, could there be anyone local who'd know about the safe? I mean, if it has been opened, it's been done with a key, and —"

I stopped. He had swung round on me, in a way that reminded me sharply of the young Davey squaring up to a fight in the school playground.

"You listen to me, Kathy Welland! I told you, if your Granddad had this put in, it would be my Grandpa he'd get to do it, and if it was meant to be private, you can bet that my Grandpa never told anyone. My Dad may know about it, because he has all the shop records, but he never told me, and he would never tell my Mum either. And if he does have a spare key —"

"Davey! It didn't occur to me! Please! Truly it didn't. Why on earth should I think any of your family would go prying about here? It really could be that Gran did this herself ages ago, to put something away or get something out, and forgot to tell me that I'd find the paper already cut away."

"Not likely." But he sounded mollified. "This wasn't done all that long ago. Look at the edges of the plaster." He was running a thumb along the cut edge as he spoke. Dry plaster-dust floated to the floor.

"Ye-es, I see. Look, Davey, if you think your father might have a key, wouldn't it be easier to wait and ask him?"

"You reckon?" And, with his sudden grin at me, we were once again on easy terms. "You'd never last till morning. We'd better find out now. Let's go right ahead and bust it open."

"All right, let's."

He set to work with the chisel, but after a while stood back, shaking his head. "The fit's too tight, I can't get the blade in for leverage. I'll really have to break it. Okay by you?"

"Yes."

It looked easy. He laid the blade of the chisel against the door's edge nearest the keyhole, and gave two sharp blows with a hammer. There was a crack, and the little door came open. Davey said something under his breath, and stood back.

"What is it?"

"Look," he said.

I looked. Predictably, but still shockingly, the safe was empty.

Davey put into words what, after his recent outburst, I didn't care to say.

"Well, so that *was* opened with a key."

"Perhaps Gran really did — oh, no, there's the plaster. Well," I said, uneasily, "it's obvious what's happened, isn't it? There's been someone in here, squatters, perhaps, dossing in the empty house, and they came across the key, wherever she left it, and tried the safe door."

"They'd have to have known it was behind the picture."

"They might just have found it if they hunted about."

"Covered over with wallpaper?"

"Oh. Well, no. Oh, dear, this is awful. What am I to say to Gran? What are we to do?"

"Better not say anything to your Gran yet. But I reckon," said Davey slowly, "that we'll have to tell Dad about this." I noticed that he had accepted my "we" as natural. "Look, I'll ask him first thing if he knew about the safe, and if there was another key, and I'll find out from Mum if that plaster on the floor was dry."

He pushed the door as far shut as it would go, then hung the Unseen Guest back in its place. "And you can forget about squatters. I've come this way on my bike two nights out of five the last month, with a job I'm doing at Swords Farm, and there's never been anyone about. And Mum would have seen signs if people had been in the house. So you don't need to be scared, but if you are —"

"I'm not. Truly. Just worried, and just wishing I could think of some explanation. I mean, if it was a thief they'd have taken the valuables, but they'd surely have left the papers, or just chucked them in the fireplace or something. Hang on a minute" — and I was on my knees, destroying Mrs Pascoe's carefully laid fire — "No, only newspaper. And they were so tidy, weren't they? They cleared most of the plaster away, and the torn wallpaper . . ." I got to my feet again. "Oh, well, there's nothing we can do for now, is there? But thanks for everything, Davey, and don't worry about me. I'll be fine, really."

"If you're sure. Good night, then."

After he had gone I sat for a while, thinking, before getting up to re-lay the fire and put a match to it. The bright blaze brought the room alive, and even made a kind of company. Home. It was a long time since I had sat by this fire, but it felt like yesterday. I got myself some supper, then found the Penguin I had bought for the train journey and read for an hour or two without thinking more than fifty times about the empty safe, and finally, when the grandmother clock said eleven, went up to bed.

8

Next morning I was up very early, but had barely finished my coffee when I heard the sound of trotting hoofs coming down the lane from the road.

I went out to meet the farmer, a wiry middle-aged man with a face carved out of sunburned teak, who jumped down from the cart and came up the path carrying his wire basket of milk-bottles.

" 'Morning. Nice to see you back. How're you keeping?"

"Good morning, Mr Blaney. I'm fine, thanks. And you?"

"Mustn't grumble. And Mrs Welland?"

"She's had flu, but she's mending. I'll tell her you asked."

"You do that. How many?"

"Do I have a choice? We're rationed in town."

"Not here, you're not. A pint do? And two-three fresh eggs if it suits you? I've got some in the cart. And I've got your suitcase there, too. I picked it up at the station. Mr Harbottle said I might as well being it down home for you."

(Home? *I remember, I remember.* But I was only here in passing, to pack up and then abandon the house where I was born, however much it seemed to want to wrap me around with familiar things. I had a job, a place elsewhere that I would soon go back to. There was nothing here for me now, not for Kate Herrick.)

I thanked Mr Blaney, and accepted his offer of eggs, while he asked a bit more about Gran and her new house (how had he heard that?) and whether or not she meant ever to come back to Todhall. He seemed to be in no hurry, and I saw why. His mare, left to herself in the lane, had trotted on to where it widened near the bridge, and there, with a couple of expert heaves of her rump, she turned the cart neatly and came back to the gate, ready for the return journey.

"She hasn't forgotten her old round, then," I said.

"Rosy? Never forgets anything. Dunno how I'd do without her. If I was to miss a call on my round, she'd take me back there and refuse to shift till I'd done it. Dear knows what I'll do when she gets her cards."

"She must be pretty old now? I remember her — oh, for years back."

"She'll be about seventeen. What I reckon, when she looks like going, I'll get myself one of those motor vans. I can't see myself starting over again with a new horse."

"And Rosy?"

He was offhand, turning away. "I reckon she's earned her retirement. She'll finish her life at grass."

"I'm so glad. I hope she knows!"

He laughed, not attempting now to conceal the affection in his voice. "Wouldn't surprise me. If she didn't before, she does now. Look at her. Hears every word. I'll get the eggs for you, and fetch your case up. No, it's no bother."

He started down the path, but, I could see, without much hope of getting near the cart. The old mare was standing with her forefeet inside the cottage gate, blocking the way, and staring fixedly, ears pricked, towards me. Mr. Blaney paused and turned, trying to sound apologetic. "I told you she never forgot. Mrs Welland used to give her a piece — a bun or a bit of bread."

"Oh, dear. Of course! I should have remembered. Would a biscuit do?"

"She wouldn't say no. Come up, lass." He backed Rosy up a pace, heaved my case out of the cart and carried it up to the door.

I took it from him. "Thanks very much. I'll get that biscuit now. How much for the milk and the eggs, Mr Blaney? I may only be here for three or four days, so perhaps I'd better pay as I go."

"Never mind that. You can let me know the day before you leave."

"I wondered — could you give me a lift up to the village, please?"

"Well, of course. Like old times, that'll be."

So it would. I thanked him again, and hurried back indoors, snatched up my jacket and the basket and purse I had left ready, found a biscuit among what remained of my stores, and ran out. As I shut the front door I hesitated. We had never locked it, but perhaps now —? I locked it, pocketed the key, then delivered the biscuit to Rosy, who took it with velvet lips, tossed her head, and was away with the milk-cart almost before I could jump aboard.

The road to the village ran, deep between its flowering hedges, through a mile or so of pasture and woodland. The only dwellings on the way were two small houses, just too big to be called cottages, which nestled at the edge of a wood. They were still occupied (Mr Blaney shouted it above the rattling of the cart) by the same people. A pair of sisters, the Miss Popes, lived in the first house, with next door a single maiden lady, Miss Linsey. The village had dubbed the place Spinsters' Corner.

Rosy stopped at the first gate, and Mr Blaney got out. There was no sign that anyone was about yet, for which I was thankful. I remembered the Miss Popes as being deeply interested in all that went on in the village; at least, that was how they would have put it; the village called them, briefly and with adjectives that varied according to the station of the speaker, interfering old tabbies. This may have been true in a sense, but Miss Mildred, the younger sister, interfered only with the kindest possible motives. One gathered that the elderly sisters had been brought up in an era of soup and advice for the deserving poor. In spite of my mother's dubious goings-on, our family had been in that category, and sometimes glad of it, but even so I had always liked Miss Mildred, whose gentle charity of mind had even included Aunt Betsy. The older sister was a more practical character, and indeed held down some sort of key post with a charitable organisation in Sunderland.

Rosy moved on to the second gate, and put her head down to the roadside grass. No biscuit expected here, and the curtains were still drawn. Miss Linsey's house. Miss Linsey was in a different category from the ladies next door. She was a mystic. She was to be seen communing (as she would tell you) with the trees and the clouds, and she laid claim to a fairly powerful kind of second sight. As a child, I had been afraid of her, and on the way home from school had always run like the wind till I was well past her doorway. We children had had our own name for Spinsters' Corner, a name which carried its own terror; we called it Witches' Corner.

Soon we were trotting briskly past the cemetery wall, to pause at the first of the outlying houses of the village. I thanked Mr Blaney for the lift, patted Rosy, who ignored me, biscuitless as I was, then I walked briskly across the village green towards my first port of call, the vicarage.

Todhall village was a community of about two hundred souls, gathered round a village green with the church at its centre. It boasted one pub, the Black Bull, a post office, a general shop, the vicarage with the smithy close by, and above the smithy the carpenter's workshop which belonged to Mr Pascoe. To either side of the green the houses straggled in no sort of order, so that what we called Front Street was in fact a wide oval of green set about with a sprawl of dwellings, gardens and small-holdings. The only modern touches (and therefore, perhaps, the less picturesque features of the place) were at the southern end of the village where the milk-cart had set me down —

the school and the church hall, with the raw brick wall of the cemetery alongside. The church, the proper centre-piece of the village picture, was late Norman, with (as I had known all my life, without understanding why it mattered) all the right stonework and a perfect horseshoe chancel arch. There were wild roses sprawling over the stone wall that surrounded the old graveyard, and some lovely elms lending their shade. A couple of goats and a donkey were tethered grazing on the green, and a gaggle of white geese sunned themselves near the pond.

As it was in the beginning . . . Nothing seemed to have changed. Nothing ever would. And, as I had done so often in the past, I made straight for the vicarage gate.

Nothing had changed there either, except that here, certainly, the house did not seem the huge mansion it had appeared when the Lockwoods had lived there, and little Kathy Welland had first gone to play with the vicar's daughter. It was a low, compact house, squarely built but made attractive with whitewashed walls and green window-shutters and a trellised porch covered with jasmine. The garden walls were almost completely hidden by ivy, and as I passed the front gate with its glimpse of a pretty garden, a blackbird flew scolding out of a tangle of leaves where, as I knew, there had been a nest every year, time out of mind.

The front gate was not, had never been, my way in. I pushed open the back gate and went into the yard where the motor house stood, and beside it the hen-run, and the cage where Prissy had kept her rabbits. The rabbits had gone, but the hens were there, busy still over the morning feed. I would have lingered for a minute, remembering, but there was someone at the scullery window, and she had seen me. As I reached the back door it opened, and a girl looked at me inquiringly, wiping her hands on her apron.

She was, I supposed, about sixteen. I did not recognize her, nor, obviously, she me.

"Oh, miss. Did you ring at the front? I'm sorry, I never heard no bell —"

"No, I didn't try the front. It's all right. I know I'm early, but is the vicar in, please? It's Mr Winton Smith, isn't it?"

"That's right, miss. But he went out a

bit since, visiting up the village. Mrs Foster at the post office. She's been poorly. But Mrs Winton Smith's down the garden somewhere. Shall I get her, or maybe you'd like to go yourself? It's through that gate by the hens."

I hesitated. "No, I'll come back later. When do you think he'll be home?"

"I couldn't say. Sometimes he stays out till dinner, that's at twelve o'clock. But I'll tell him you came — what name is it, miss?"

"Herrick, Mrs Herrick. I think he'll know who I am. So I may see you later. What's your name, by the way?"

"I'm Lil Ashby."

The Ashbys were farmers a few miles along beyond the station. I remembered Mrs Ashby, who had called sometimes on Gran, and had supplied the Hall, and us along with it, with eggs and poultry.

"Well, Lily, thanks for your help."

"It's not really Lily. It's Lil, short for Lilias. Mum called me after someone she knew. Real pretty, she said, like the name." A cheerful giggle. "And the name's the prettiest thing about me, she says that, too.

What is it, miss. Is there summat the matter?"

"No, no. Yes, it's a very pretty name,
and it suits you. Well, then, tell the vicar,
and I'll be back later. Goodbye."

Outside the gate I paused. A little way
to the right a farmer's cart stood upended
by the road, shafts in the air. The horse
was presumably in the smithy being shod.
I could hear the clink of the hammer and
the clatter of hoofs and a "Hup there!"
from the smith.

I went that way. I had always loved the
smithy. To me, as a child, it had been a
mysterious dark cave, with the fire at the
back roaring up from time to time under
the bellows, and the rhythmic clang and
clatter of hammer and anvil mixing with
the hiss of the iron plunged to cool and
the smell of the smoking hoof as the
shoe was tried. I had loved it all; the old
smith with his leather apron and hard
hands that could be so gentle; the great
mild horses, their skins as glossy as
licked toffee, their quiet eyes, the way
they heaved their feet up at a word and
never seemed to feel nail or hot iron,
their soft flickering nostrils that nuzzled

and breathed down the smith's neck as he worked. A whole world. A world whose ways, sadly, must soon vanish for ever.

The smith was busy over the hind hoof of an enormous Clydesdale, his back wedged under the chestnut rump, his knees gripping the powerful leg. He shot a glance upward as my shadow paused in the doorway and spat out a nail to let him grunt something that sounded like, "Nice mornin'."

"Good morning, Mr Corner."

Another glance, as he tapped in the last nail, then he checked the shoe's hold, lowered the horse's leg, patted the chestnut flank, and straightened himself. "Well, if it isn't little Kathy Welland! Long time since you were in these parts. Your Granny here with you?"

"No. She's still in Scotland, and I think she'll stay there now. She sent me down to get the rest of her things from the cottage."

"Ah. Well, I'm sorry to hear that, but it's nice to have you home again. You be here long?"

"Only till I get Gran's things seen to. It's

lovely to be back. Everything looks just the same. How's Mrs Corner?"

"Fine, fine. What about your Granny? Annie Pascoe said she hadn't been too clever."

"That's right. She's on the mend now, but she's feeling her age, she says."

"Then I'd best be watching out for mine," said the smith with a bark of laughter. "Ah, here you are, Jem. She's ready now, done all round, and that should keep her for a canny bit."

I waited while the young man — a stranger to me — settled with the smith and led the mare away, then said: "I was wanting to see Mr Pascoe. Is he upstairs in the shop?"

"Nay, lass. Him and Davey, they've been and gone. They're working up to the Hall. There's a lot of alteration there, turning the place into a hotel, but you'll likely know that."

"Yes, I did hear. I saw Davey yesterday. I wanted to ask you — do you make keys, or is it only big things, gates and such?"

"Anything in iron, I can make," said Mr Corner simply. "But keys? They don't come my way often. I once made a spare

for the church tower when old Tom Pink-
erton — you'll remember him, he's still
sexton — dropped her down the well. A
big old key that was, near as old as the
church."

"This would be a small key, very small,
a bit like a cash box key, I would think.
No? Then what about a door key, the old-
fashioned sort, quite big. Like this." I
showed him the Rose Cottage key. "I
wondered if anyone had asked you to
make one lately?"

He regarded me for a moment under
those bushy eyebrows, but said merely:
"Nay, lass. Anything like that, they'd go to
a locksmith. Baines in Durham's the nearest."

"I see. Thanks. Well, you're busy, and
I'd better be going. It's lovely to see you
again, Mr Corner."

"Good to see you, lass, and if you was
dressed for it I'd give you a job the way
I used to, you and young Pris. You been
to the vicarage? Thought I saw you come
out, but I didn't know you, my eyes not
being what they used to be at a distance."

"I was wanting to see the vicar, but he's

out. The garden looks nice. Is Mrs Winton Smith the gardener?"

"Aye. Always at it, she is. Well, if I cannat set you to work, I'll be getting on myself. I've a wheel to fettle next door." Next door was the shed where he did his wheelwright's work. "Come back and see me before you go, lass. Or better still, come up to the house and get a cup of tea. The missus'd be real pleased to see you. Any day about six, and I can run you home in the trap."

"That would be lovely. Thanks very much."

And at any time after six o'clock today, I reckoned, as I went out into the sunshine, everyone in Todhall would know that Kathy Welland was down home at Rose Cottage, packing up her grandmother's things to send away to Scotland, and asking about keys. Like any other village, we had a very efficient grapevine. So, I would use it for myself. Perhaps someone, somewhere, might know if anyone had been hanging around Rose Cottage and might have broken in and rifled Gran's safe of her treasures.

9

The village shop lay about a hundred yards beyond the smithy, and looked out across the duckpond. The geese had left the water, and were marching purposefully across the green towards a farmyard we had always known as Scurr's, though it had been many years since anyone called Scurr had lived there. Their place on the water had been taken by a small fleet of ducks, mostly white Aylesburys, but with a visiting mallard in convoy, and one water-hen. A nondescript terrier sat at the edge of the water, wistfully eyeing the flotilla.

A shrill whistle from just behind me jerked me round, startled, and jerked the terrier, too, from his post. He came running to the shop doorway, which had opened to let a young woman — a girl of about sixteen — out onto the step.

She saw me and stopped in the doorway. "Oh, sorry! I never saw you. Come

here, Muffin! You leave them ducks alone!
Were you coming in the shop? He'd love
to get them ducks, but he's frightened of
the water. You can't blame him, can you,
all that mud and the weed and all. A fair
disgrace I call it, and no one does a thing
about it. Come in, then. I'm Jinnie Barlow,
Mrs Barlow's niece, from Ashhurst, and
keeping the shop while she's on holiday. I
haven't met you yet, have I?"

"No. I'm Kate Herrick. Nice to meet
you, Jinnie. Will Mrs Barlow be away
long?"

"Only a week. She's gone over to Har-
tlepool, to her sister's, my other Aunty's.
She's just out of hospital, my other Aunty,
that is, so I said I'd come and mind the
shop, and the cat and dog. The shop's
the least of the troubles." She laughed
merrily. "Whose are the ducks?"

"I don't know. They probably belong to
Scurr's, like the geese. I think they're used
to dogs — anyway, I'm sure they'll know
Muffin quite well. I wouldn't worry about
them."

"I won't. What can I get you, then? Is
it the rations?"

"Yes, please. here's the book."

"Ta. Makes it easy, this does. This is only my second day, and I've not quite got the hang of Aunty's shelves yet, but the rations are easy, and I've got some of them made up ready anyway."

She chattered on as she served me. Ashhurst, where she lived, was about five miles away, and before this visit, she told me, she had done no more than call occasionally on her aunt, but she was enjoying this temporary job because one of her friends from home was working at the vicarage.

"Lil Ashby?" I said. "Yes, of course. Their farm's over Ashhurst way. You'd be at school with her?"

I spoke absently, watching all the while through the glass of the door to see if I could catch a glimpse of the vicar coming away from his call on Mrs Foster at the post office on the other side of the green. Mrs Barlow's absence was disappointing. She was a great gossip, and since most people who visited the village found their way at some time to the shop, I had hoped she might have some information for me.

"That it?" asked Jinnie, putting the last

of the packages into my basket. "We've got some tins of Spam, if you'd like one, and what about flour?"

"Oh, no thanks. I've got all I need, and I don't want a lot to carry. It's a long way to Rose Cottage. This'll do me very well. How much is it?"

She told me and I paid her. As she counted out the change she asked, with the first sign of curiosity, "Rose Cottage? Isn't that the place away down the station road? Where the old lady died and the sister went up north to stay? I heard about that."

I hesitated, then put the question I had wanted to ask Mrs Barlow. "Did your aunt say if there'd been any strangers seen about there lately, or maybe asking about it?"

"Not that I remember. Here, don't forget your ration book." As she handed it to me she caught sight of the address on the cover. "Richmond, Surrey? Oh, you're not from Todhall, then? And you're lodging down at Rose Cottage? On your own? Isn't it lonesome there?"

"Not really." There was the vicar now, shutting Mrs Foster's gate and setting out to cross the green. He appeared to be making for the church.

"Are you just there on holiday, then? Related, maybe? Aunty did tell me —"

"Excuse me. Someone I want to see. I must catch him. Thanks again, Jinnie. Good morning." Snatching my basket up I made hastily for the door, tripping over Muffin, who was waiting to be let out again, presumably for further contemplation of the ducks. In the ensuing scuffle as he was caught and held and apologised for, I made my escape from further questions and headed back down the green towards the church.

When I let myself in through the south door, there was no sign of the vicar. A woman was there, below the pulpit, with a bucket full of flowers and branches beside her, and a couple of big brass vases on the floor waiting to be filled. I recognised the massive vases that stood to either side of the chancel arch. On festival days my grandfather used to bring boughs of blossom or leaves from the

Hall grounds. For ordinary Sundays the vases usually had to stand empty.

The church, the eternal centre of the village, was unchanged, not shrunken like Rose Cottage and the vicarage. The same yesterday, today and for ever. Just as it should be. I supposed — fleetingly, as I slipped into a back pew to say the brief prayer that was one's civil greeting to the church's owner — that the timelessness was the quality all churches shared; a matter admittedly, to some extent, of shadows and carvings and high groined ceilings and dim religious light, but also of the years of use, the words, the thoughts, the griefs and joys of countless people through the years. Here in Todhall there had been some nine centuries of them.

I got to my feet and approached the flower-arranger. She had not looked round as I entered the church, but now she stood up and greeted me. She was tall, thin rather than slender, with brown hair that showed a hint of grey tucked back uncaringly under a felt hat. She looked to be somewhere in her sixties, and wore an elderly skirt topped by a cardigan over a white shirt blouse. She greeted me with a poise verging on condescension. Her voice was educated.

"Good morning. A lovely day, isn't it? Are you interested in our church?"

"Good morning. You must be Mrs Winton Smith?"

"Yes?"

It was a question, and she waited for an answer. I said: "I'm Kate Herrick, Mrs Herrick. I called at the vicarage earlier, but the vicar was out. There's something I'm rather anxious to ask him about, and I thought I might catch him here. I was over there in the shop just now and saw him come across the green. I suppose he's come in by the vestry door? Do you think I might go in there and have a word with him?"

"I didn't hear the door, but he may be there, he did say something about looking out some papers this morning, and I do know that he is very busy. But" — she was gracious — "perhaps there is something I can do for you? You're a stranger to the village, aren't you? If it's the church you're interested in, there's a very good booklet written by the last vicar. It's down there on the bench by the font. I'm afraid we charge threepence, but churches do have expenses."

She must be practised, I thought, at defending her husband against time-wasters. I had to find some way through the defences. I looked down at the bucketful of flowers. "What lovely flowers. Do you grow them yourself?"

"Yes. They're all from the vicarage garden. Are you a gardener, Mrs Herrick?"

I smiled. "In a way. I work for a nursery firm in Richmond."

"Are you visiting friends here?"

"I'm just here for a day or two. Staying at Rose Cottage. You must know it, it's down —"

"Oh yes, I know it." She had stooped over a vase again, and now looked up. "But surely you're not there alone? Aren't you nervous?"

"Not a bit. You're the second person today who's asked me that. Why should I be?"

"All I know is, when my grandchildren came to stay for their half-term, they wouldn't go near the place. Someone had told them it was haunted."

"Haunted?"

"Yes. I don't know who by, something to do with gipsies. They used to camp there, I believe, and they were something to do with the people at Rose Cottage, some dreadful family that lived there, and some scandalous goings-on. Before our time, of course, the scandal, that is. Welland, that was the name. Welland."

A conversation-stopper if ever there was one. And that was the moment when the vicar chose to come bustling out through the vestry door. In sharp, and rather unkind, contrast to his wife he was a chubby, kindly-looking man with a thick mop of white hair and bright blue eyes peering over a pair of half-moon spectacles with gold rims, which had slid almost to the end of his nose.

He pushed them up absently, and they slid down again. "Ah, Muriel. I thought I heard voices," he said, and then to me: "Good morning. A beautiful day, isn't it? A beautiful day."

"This is Mrs Herrick," said his wife. "She is visiting the village, and is interested in the church, and I think she wanted to talk to you about it, but I told her that this was a busy day for you, Wednesday, with the evening service to prepare for, and —"

She was interrupted. The vicar came hurrying down the chancel steps with his hand out in greeting. "Mrs Herrick? Mrs Herrick, is it? How do you do? How do you do? I was speaking with Lady Brandon on the telephone only yesterday, and she mentioned that you were coming to visit your old haunts. Indeed, indeed. So, you wish to talk to me? Of course, a pleasure. If you like to come over to the vicarage now we can talk there." He turned to his wife. "Mrs Herrick, my dear, must know this church better than either you or I. Her folk have lived here for a very long time. She was a Welland before her marriage. Kathy Welland, wasn't it, from Rose Cottage?"

I said nothing. Mrs Winton Smith said nothing. The vicar said: "Shall we go?" which seemed an excellent suggestion. We went.

10

The vicar's study was much as I remembered it, a small room to the right of the front door, with a bow window from which, sitting at his desk, he could see who was approaching the house. Beyond the ivied wall of the front garden the church tower seemed very near.

There was a fire laid, but not lighted, in the grate. Above the mantelpiece hung a large engraving of an Oxford college, and on the mantelpiece itself were two silver cups and a college crest mounted on a wooden base. The other walls were lined with bookcases. It would have served nicely, I thought, for a stage set of "clergyman's study". It looked, in fact, exactly the same as it had in his predecessor's time, save that Prissy's father had been to Cambridge, and there had been an oar hung above one of the bookcases. There were even the same two baggy leather armchairs. Mr Winton Smith gestured me to one, himself taking the swivel chair at the desk, whirling it so that he faced into the room. Probably a practised manoeuvre; it put him with his back to the window, and on a higher level than his visitor. Understandable; this room must have seen quite a few difficult or delicate interviews.

But I didn't see that this would be one of them. Nor, apparently, did he. He picked up a box of cigarettes, offered me one, and when I shook my head said, "Wise girl," smiled, and took one himself.

I opened the batting. "You said you had spoken with Lady Brandon, vicar, and that she told you I was coming here to Todhall?"

"That is so. Yes. I understood from her that you were to stay at Rose Cottage, and that she had asked Mrs Pascoe to open it up for you. I trust all is well there? It has been empty a long time."

"It's fine, thank you. I don't — that is, I didn't — expect to be here more than a couple of days."

"Indeed, indeed?" A look, disconcertingly quick, over the top of his glasses.

"Does that mean that you plan now to stay longer?"

"I may have to. There's something — that's why I came to see you. Did Lady Brandon tell you what I was here for?"

"Certainly. She said that your grand-mother had decided to stay in Scotland and make her home there, and had asked you to come here to clear the cottage and arrange for the rest of her furniture to be sent north. I must say, Mrs Herrick, that I was sorry to hear it. Your grandmother was a great character, a great character, and I always enjoyed my visits there."

"She wasn't a very great churchgoer — at least I don't remember it." I smiled. "She used to pack me off, though, regular as clockwork, church, Sunday School, the lot, but she hardly ever went with me. Aunt Betsy did, though, sometimes."

"Ah. Yes. A worthy lady," said the vicar cautiously.

His expression of reserve was so marked that I laughed. "Don't say you didn't know that she used to sit outside in the church-yard till the service was over, in case the true faith — hers, that is — was contaminated? Surely someone would tell you — in fact I'll bet she told you herself!"

"And you would win. She, ah, she tended to make her opinions very clear. But at least you say she brought you, and fairly regularly, too."

"Only because she wanted to make sure i didn't have any fun — that is, get into mischief."

Another of those shrewd glimmers from above the half-moon glasses. "Indeed, indeed. The sins of children. Well, you were going to tell me why you were planning to stay longer. I hope there's nothing wrong? I believe you said that all was well at the cottage?"

"All's well with me, certainly. But a worrying thing has happened. There were a few small things that Gran had put away in a private hidey-hole, and they've gone."

"Gone?"

"Disappeared. Been taken. Things she specially asked me to take back to her."

"Oh, dear. I'm sorry to hear that. How very disturbing. I take it you've had a thorough search?"

"Not yet, no. But they should still have

been where she'd hidden them, and there's no sign of them."

"Your grandmother couldn't have been mistaken? Forgotten just where they were?"

"It's not very likely. This was a secure, locked cupboard, built into the wall, and papered over, and she'd hidden the key away somewhere. She *had* forgotten where that was, and I haven't had time yet to look for it, but when I saw the cupboard last night it had been uncovered. Someone had cut back the wallpaper and the plaster to clear the door, and the cupboard was empty."

"Dear me. This is bad, very bad. Does it mean — do you think that the thieves had found the key?"

"They must have done. They had certainly used a key. They'd taken everything, and locked the cupboard again."

"It was locked? But if you yourself had no key —?"

"I broke it open. At least Davey did. Davey Pascoe. He was with me. Finding the wall stripped like that, we had to see if Gran's goods were still there, and it was the only way."

"Yes. Yes, I see. Well, I really am sorry to hear this, Mrs Herrick." A pause, while he swivelled his chair to face the window, then swung back to me. "The missing items. How valuable are they?"

"Intrinsically, not very. Things like medals and a ring or two and a brooch, small value, but the sort of thing you don't want to lose. I suppose the most valuable item was five gold sovereigns. Apart from that it was mostly family papers, you know, birth certificates, marriage lines, all the things one keeps."

"I see. Yes, I see. How very upsetting. Have you any — well, suspicions as to what may have happened?"

"None. The only people with any right of access to the cottage are the Pascoes, and they're hardly suspects. The family, too, of course — the Brandons, I mean — but you could say the same for them, and anyway they're not here."

"Hm." He stubbed his cigarette out, frowned down at the ash for a moment, then turned back to me. "I take it there's something you want me to do? If I can help you, of course I will, though I don't quite see how."

"I was going to ask you if you'd heard of anyone who'd been seen hanging around the cottage, a tramp, perhaps, or some other stranger. But you'd have told me already if you had. So all I can do for the moment is ask if you would — oh, there is one thing, have the gipsies ever been back? They used to camp in the lonnon not far from the house, but for years before I left they'd never been there. Has there been any sign of them?"

"None. I know the lane, and it's been overgrown ever since I came here. But you were going to let me know what I can do for you?"

"Yes, please. I wondered if you would let me look at the parish registers? All the family records must be there in the church, mustn't they?"

"Some of them, certainly. Not the records of birth, of course. Those — and the deaths — would be at Somerset House. They would supply copies of the certificates if you wanted them. I can give you the address to write to."

"Thank you, I already have it. But you'll have records of the baptisms and funerals

and marriages — one does get a certificate of baptism, doesn't one?"

"Why, certainly," he said, and from the
gentleness of his tone it was apparent
that he, like his wife, had heard all there
was to hear about the dreadful Welland
family. But his reaction was different, and
not, I thought, a purely professional one.
"Of course you may look at the books.
But we can do more than that. I can make
copies for you of all the entries relating to
your family. Those losses need not worry
you. I'll do it with pleasure."

"Can you really? I didn't know. Thank
you very much."

"I wish I could do more. Regarding the
other items, the brooches and so on —
your neighbours, I would have thought,
would be the ones to talk to. The Misses
Pope" — the suspicion of a smile " —
don't miss many of the village comings
and goings. They may have seen something."

"Yes, I'd thought of them. I'll call in today." I returned the smile. "And perhaps
Miss Linsey may be guided for me."

"Indeed, indeed." His favourite exclama-
tion was obviously a cover for thought.

Once more he swivelled the chair half round and back again to face me. "What I might suggest, under the circumstances . . . Would you like me to have a word with Bob Crawley?"

"Bob Crawley? I don't think — who's he?"

"Since your time. Our policeman. Old Mr Bainbridge retired two years ago. He went to live with his daughter at Ferryhill. Bob Crawley has his house now, you'll know the one, the police house up at Lane Ends. If it would make it easier for you —?" He paused on a question-mark.

"Oh, yes, thank you. Thank you very much. If you would? Now I've taken up enough of your time, and I know how busy you are — I gather that you still have a service on Wednesday evenings — you do? Then thank you again for seeing me. About the copies of the certificates — when would it be convenient for me to come back?"

He got to his feet as I rose. "The easiest thing would be if you could make a list, with dates, of the papers you think have disappeared. Can you ask your grandmother? No, I can see that you don't want to have to trouble her before you've had time to find out more about this business. Well, then, just the records that you know would be held here in the church, weddings and funerals and yes, we do record baptisms. If you can let me have the dates of those, it will save a lot of searching. Where do you suppose they start?"

"I'm not sure. I suppose with Gran's wedding, and I can't remember just what year — oh, I've had an idea. If it's still there, she had an old photo album, and the dates might be in that. If I look tonight — is there a time tomorrow when I could let you have them?"

"If you send the list up with the milk-cart, then I can have the pages found if you come to see me later on. I've a christening at" — he glanced down at a diary on the desk — "yes, at four o'clock. So, half past three, say, at the church?"

"Thank you, that'll be great. I'll see you get the list first thing."

As I crossed to the door I glanced out of the window just in time to see the front gate open, and Mrs Winton Smith, back from the church with her empty trug, let-

ting herself into the garden. I braced myself to meet her, but she managed, with
perfect dignity, to vanish round the side of
the house just as her husband ushered
me out of the front door.

Two faces saved. But I wondered, as I
let myself out through the gate into the
sunny roadway, why I cared, and for
whom I was doing the caring. Lilias? Aunt
Betsy? Gran? Myself?

Lilias, from all I knew or had heard of her,
would not have cared a rap. Besides, she
was dead. Aunt Betsy had certainly cared,
quite terribly, but she was dead, too. Gran
had lived with the slur of "shame" all too
long, and was now a long way away.
Which left me. I had cared as a child, when
people had let slip in my hearing remarks
about my mother, or had too openly pitied
my fatherless state. At school I had had to
bear the thoughtless questions of the other
children, and sometimes teasing, but this
had come to an end on the day when Billy
Comstock, the ten-year-old bully from
Lane Ends, had found a new word, "bas-
tard", and tried it out in school playtime,
until Davey, aged nine, had flown at him
and fought him till he yelled for help, and

the two of them, streaming with blood, had to be pulled apart by the teacher. I was never teased again.

But that was a long time ago, and I had, perforce, worked out my own philosophy of living. It had to be what you were, not who you were, that mattered. I had taken life as it was dealt me, loved my home, and been happy. Would be happy again. So the person to be sorry for here was Mrs Winton Smith, a snob who had dropped a social brick, and who, being what she was, would obviously care very much about that.

Muffin was sitting by the pond again, but I doubted if he would be there for very long. The geese were on their way back from Scurr's yard, and the gander did not suffer dogs or children gladly. I would have liked to linger to watch the confrontation, but there was a lot to do. I turned for home.

11

The younger Miss Pope, Miss Mildred, was busy in her garden when I got to Witches' Corner. She was almost always busy in her garden, which was immaculately kept and extremely pretty, though Miss Mildred knew little or nothing about gardening methods, or even about plants. I had heard my grandfather talking often enough about her — "a real green thumb, that one has, and not knowing what on earth to do with it." The comment had stemmed from the time when he had stopped at her gate to ask her about some plant, a rareish species, which was growing rampant on her garden wall, and her reply, full of enthusiasm, had been, "That pink thing? What did you say it was? I've always called it my dear little rockery plant."

"She never prunes her roses, either," Granddad had said, "and look at them! Real beauties, all of them, and flowering two full weeks before mine at the Hall. Where's the justice?" Then he had laughed, starting to fill his awful old pipe, and said indulgently, "But there, it's a matter of love. Beats manure any day, that does."

But by whatever method or lack of it, Miss Mildred's garden was enchanting, a real cottage garden full of all the things it should have held, delphiniums, lupins, pinks and violas, with roses and honeysuckle on the rampage on every surface they could find. The house and garden were purely Miss Mildred's territory; her elder sister Agatha was the man of the house, the breadwinner, travelling by train daily to Sunderland to her work.

When I paused at the garden gate Miss Mildred was visible only as a flowered cotton rump sticking up among the lupins. I opened the gate and called her name, and she up-ended to her full five feet three inches, peered out between the lupins (which were taller than she was), and then broke out into delighted exclamations.

"It's Kathy! Well, my goodness, if it isn't little Kathy Welland!" She was a dumpy little creature, with the pink cheeks and blue eyes of a long-faded prettiness, and wispy grey hair that was rather the worse for its morning among the lupins. "Come in, my dear, come in! How lovely to see you! Annie Pascoe said you were coming, and here you are! It's like a miracle!"

Briefly wondering if this made Mrs Pascoe a liar or a prophet, I accepted Miss Mildred's fervent double handclasp and feather-light kiss and let myself be drawn into the garden, to answer as best I could all her eager questions about Gran, the family at the Strathbeg house, and then myself, my war work and marriage, and my life in London since my husband's death. It was a demonstration of what the village said, that "the Miss Popes knew the inside of everything." One could see how, but the eager questions were so full of real interest, with a total lack of criticism or any shade of unkindness, that one found oneself answering readily and in detail. As Granddad had said of her garden, with Miss Mildred it was a matter of love. There was about her a rare and genuine innocence — in the most literal meaning of the word — that made it impossible to take offense, however personal her questions and comments.

"So you were left nicely off, well, that's a mercy, isn't it? I mean, that's *something* . . . And what a lovely job you've got, working with flowers. I suppose" — with an absent eye on the lily-buds shouldering their way up through carnations and roses — "they get all sorts of special flowers in those big London places? Flown in from Africa and India and the South Sea Islands and such-like?"

"Yes, they do. Some of them are lovely, but not a patch on yours, Miss Mildred! Your garden's gorgeous, it really is, just as I remember it."

"Well, we're having such a beautiful summer." Having so to speak passed the credit on, she turned back to me. "Are you here for long? You must come and have supper with us when my sister's home. She won't want to miss you."

"I'd love it, if I can, but I don't quite know yet how long I'll be here. Mrs Pascoe would surely tell you what I'd come?"

It was a very mild shaft, and it went wide. "Oh yes, she told me all about it. And she says that Jim and Davey will help you, and I suppose they'll get Caslaw's to do the move. Which bit does she want, your grandmother? She'll want the old sideboard, I'm sure, and the rocking-chair, and is the table hers, and the other chairs? It'll be nice for her to have all her own things around her again." A pause and a quick intake of breath. "Oh, goodness, of course —"

"What is it?" I asked, as she stopped.

"So stupid of me to forget, but seeing you suddenly like this, and then the garden, always so much to be done . . . I meant to come and tell you, but now you're here . . . Come over here and we'll sit down." She led the way to a seat set back under a rustic arch predictably laden with pink rambling roses laced through with purple clematis. We sat.

"It was talking about your grandmother's furniture and things that reminded me, though how I could have forgotten I don't know. Sister said I must tell you if I saw you, but I did wonder if it would scare you, staying down there alone at the cottage."

She paused, looking a little anxious. I said quickly, "Being alone doesn't scare me. Really it doesn't. Do go on."

"Well, if you're sure . . . It was Monday, just the day before you got here. Sister had told me she would get home late, because there'd been a muddle at the office, with someone being ill the week before, so she would get the later train, and she would bring the papers home to do in the evening. And she goes to the market on a Monday as a rule and gets what we need for the week, things you can't get in the village or from Barlow's van. So I knew she'd have a lot to carry, and there isn't usually anyone else getting off here from that train, so I thought I'd walk down to the station to meet her. Well, I was a bit late starting, so when I got to the Rose Cottage lane-end I thought I might take the short cut by Gipsy Lonnen. It was getting dark by then — just dusk, really — but I know the way so well, and it does save a lot of time."

Another pause. I prodded gently. "So you went by the lonnen?"

"No. I didn't get as far as the stile. I was about half way down the lane from the road when I saw it. At least, I think I saw it, but Sister says —"

"Saw what, Miss Mildred?"

"A light in your cottage garden. Round the back. A light that moved."

I stirred. "Well, but couldn't it just have been Mrs Pascoe? She's been coming down from the Hall when the men were working there, to put the place right."

"At that hour? Anyway, Annie Pascoe goes to the Mothers' Union meeting on a Monday night, and she went that night, because I asked her. I asked her if anyone else had a key, and she said no, certainly not."

"What time was this? The last train? Could it have been reflected moonlight, maybe, from a window?"

"No. And I told you, the light moved, like someone with a torch."

I was silent for a moment. In my mind's eye I was seeing the framed text hanging on the cottage wall, with the rifled safe behind it. It was one thing to trust the vicar with the truth, but I wasn't yet ready to broadcast it to the village via Miss Mildred. So I said merely, "How horrid for you. No wonder you asked if I minded being alone there. What did you do?"

"I am not myself afraid of the dark," said Miss Mildred, "but I don't like meeting strangers in it. I knew the cottage was empty, but there was nothing there that thieves would want to take, and anyway, I didn't want to be late for Sister's train, so I went. Not by the lonnen. I went back up the lane, and to the station by the road."

"I don't blame you. But — was the light all you saw? Nobody moving about?"

"I didn't care to go close enough to look," said Miss Mildred, with dignity. "And I couldn't wait to see if anyone came round into the front garden. I had to hurry. By the time I got to the station the train had gone, and I met Sister on the road."

"Did you tell her about the light?"

"Oh, yes. She said it would be silly to go and look, but we must tell Bob Crawley. That's the policeman, he's new since you were here. Such a nice young man, and with two dear little children, twins, a boy and a girl, and so keen on his garden, Bob, I mean, not the twins, and I was able to give him a lot of nice plants when they first moved in, and he has really got it beautiful now, even though it is mostly vegetables."

"And you told him what you'd seen?"

"Yes. That is, young Freddie Smart — you'll have met him, the porter at the station — came by on his bike; he goes home after the last train, and we asked him to call at Lane Ends on his way home, and tell Bob. And Bob went down to Rose Cottage straight away. He went past while we were having supper. He went all round and he came in on his way back and said nothing was disturbed that he could see, except that someone had been digging round the back, near the toolshed. So you see, I must have been right."

"Digging?" I said blankly. It had already occurred to me that what she had seen might just have been Davey fetching the tools, but then what would he have been digging for, and after dark, too?

"That's what he said. Digging, just by the toolshed. Bob did ask Davey Pascoe about it, because he knew Davey had got your grandfather's things from the shed, but that was last week — you did know about that, dear? That your grandmother had said Davey might take the tools and things from the shed?"

"Yes, I —"

A piercing shriek startled us both to our feet. It came from behind the hedge that separated Miss Mildred's garden from the one next door, where Miss Linsey lived. As we both hurried to the hedge to see what violent crime was being committed behind it, a head appeared over the top, and said in a voice that would have made a fortune for a tragic actress, "I've found him!"

12

I had not seen Miss Linsey for some years, but she had not changed at all. She was of middle height, middle age, medium build, but nothing else about her was medium, except perhaps in the professional sense of the word. She had a thin face, with a prominent aquiline nose, and myopic, rather mad-looking eyes, and she was in the habit, probably because of the myopia, of poking her head forward and fixing you with a fiercely intent stare, much as a large hawk stares down its beak at the prey it has marked down. Her hair was pepper-and-salt, fair turning grey, and was usually frizzed out into an old-fashioned coiffure rather like a bird's nest, but just now it was straggling in a wild tangle, as she had, quite literally, been through a hedge with it. She was holding something up in both hands, and repeating in triumph, "I've found him! He was just coming back through the hedge! He's been in your garden all the time!"

"Who has?" asked Miss Mildred, looking bewildered.

"Henry! If he's had your sweet peas I'm sorry — he does so love sweet peas, and when they're so near the fence — such a temptation! I did put wire netting right along there, but he finds a way through anything. Naughty, naughty Henry! Oh hullo, is that Kathy Welland? Annie Pascoe said you were here. I'd love a little talk with you, but I can't ask you in to coffee because I've run out, and I've no biscuits, but some other time soon, perhaps —"

"Thank you, I'm on my way home now, anyway. Do tell, who is Henry?"

"Oh, well, half a mo, I'll come round. Really, Mildred, I'd have thought you'd have seen him, he's been gone nearly a week, and . . ." The voice trailed away as its owner turned and vanished once more behind the hedge. We heard the clash of her gate and then she reappeared at Miss Mildred's. She was carrying a tortoise.

"Henry?" I said.

"Yes, the naughty boy! I found him just

squeezing back through the bottom of the hedge. I was so afraid he was lost this time. If they stay out till winter, you know, they die." The light intense gaze fixed itself on me. "So you did come. They were right. I knew it. It's not always easy to tell, but this time I was sure. You must actually have been on your way at the time. It's like a miracle."

Somehow, this was a rather different sort of miracle from Miss Mildred's. I groped for some kind of sense. "What do you mean, Miss Linsey? Who were right?"

I might as well not have spoken. Waving the tortoise vaguely in the direction of the village, she went on, "And when Annie Pascoe said you'd got off the train yesterday I felt like saying, 'Well, of course,' and if she hadn't told me I would still have known it had to be you, even though you haven't been back here for all these years, and you've changed so much, a young lady now and so well spoken —"

"Bella —" Miss Mildred started a protest, but Miss Linsey was not to be put off. She waved the tortoise at her, but kept her eyes fixed on me. "You're not really at all like your mother, are you?"

"I'm sorry?"

"Oh, I don't mean to be rude. You're very good-looking, you must know that, but you're dark, and she was so fair, really golden, when she was a girl, wasn't she, Mildred?"

"Yes, but, Bella, really —"

"Of course those looks don't last, but she carries her age very well. I saw her only a few days ago."

Miss Mildred made a little movement of protest, and I said under my breath, "It's all right," adding, aloud, "when was this, Miss Linsey?"

"The other night. I forget. Nights are all the same. People come and go. Some of them are dreams, but some come back in daylight. It's hard to tell. The man who was with her — I don't know who that was. He looked like a gipsy. She went away with a gipsy, didn't she?" She paused, but not for an answer. There was no shred of malice in look or voice. She gave me a smile, making another large gesture with the long-suffering tortoise. "But you mustn't let it trouble you, my dear. There's never any need to be afraid of them. The spirits, I mean. Believe me,

I know. They only come back if they are lonely, or if they have something to tell you. They never harm anyone."

"On the other hand," said Miss Mildred, firmly bringing the conversation back to earth, "your Henry has been doing quite a lot of harm to my border. I hadn't noticed till now, but just look down there." She pointed to a patch of very pretty dwarf campanula, which certainly showed signs of damage. "Look at that! My little blue bells, I call them, and all squashed and nibbled. It must have been Henry, but perhaps the poor little soul was hungry. Why don't you take him home, Bella, and give him some of that lettuce I gave you, and then come back and have a cup of coffee here? I baked this morning."

"Just a minute," I said, stooping. Something white showed among the little blue bells, an elongated oval shape, something over an inch long, tucked in among the campanula leaves. I stood up with it in my hand. It was recognisably an egg, though strangely shaped, and with a tough-looking, matt, slightly uneven shell. I held it out on my palm. The two ladies regarded it with curiosity and slight repulsion, the tortoise with indifference.

"That's what Henry's been up to," I said. "Henrietta. She was laying an egg."

"An egg?" Miss Mildred sounded lost. "An egg? But — he's not a bird. How can he lay an egg?"

"A reptile. They lay eggs. I saw one like this once before somewhere. It's a tortoise's egg."

Miss Linsey looked from the tortoise to the egg with something like pride. "Well, would you believe that? Henry! And they leave them to hatch in the sun, don't they? Do you suppose we could actually *hatch* it? In the airing-cupboard, perhaps, or over the stove?" Quite suddenly, it seemed, Miss Linsey was back with us in the real and daylight world. She gave Miss Mildred a look where I could see a kind of indulgent affection. "Wouldn't it be fun to bring up a dear little baby tortoise? What do you think, Kathy?"

"I don't know. You could try. But — well, does Henry live on his own, or does anyone else in the village have a tortoise?"

"No, I've never heard of another one

here, and I've had him for three years. Oh, well." And Miss Linsey dropped the egg into her pocket. "All right, Mildred, thanks. I'll take him — it's far too difficult to say 'her' all of a sudden — I'll take him home to his pen, and I'd love some coffee, thank you." Then to me, "You'll be staying, too, Kathy?"

"I can't. I must get back, but I hope I'll see you again before I leave. Perhaps —" But she had already disappeared back to her own garden. We could hear her admonishing Henry as she went.

"Er — Kathy, my dear," said Miss Mildred, low-voiced, "what she was saying about your poor mother — all that was just her way, you know. It doesn't mean anything. She sees things. She was telling me just the other day that our dear father had been here, working in the garden, and you know he's been gone for nearly fifteen years, and he never was a great gardener. I don't know if you remember how she talks sometimes —"

"Yes, I do." I also remembered what I had heard about the old tyrant of a father who had never lifted a spade in his life, and who had been lovingly cared for by his daughters until any chance of living their own lives was long past. I said gently, "I know. Just one of her dreams. Don't worry. It didn't matter."

"That's all right, then." Relieved, she turned the subject, moving with me towards the gate. "Well, my dear, if you must go. How very strange about Henry, isn't it? The egg, I mean. And wouldn't it be nice — and kind to dear little Henry, too — to try and hatch it? Do you think perhaps one of Mrs Blaney's hens — I'm sure she said she has a broody just now."

"I don't think it would hatch. If there's no other tortoise in the village —"

"What difference does that make?"

A startled glance at her kind, inquiring face, and I fell back on a cowardly kind of truth. "The hen wouldn't sit long enough. They take ages, tortoises. It — well, believe me, Miss Mildred, it wouldn't work."

"Oh? What a pity. Ah, well. Now don't you worry about Bella's dreams and visions. She does get so mixed up. She's a dear girl, but you could say a little *unworldly*. You really can't stay for coffee?"

"No, thank you. There are things I've

got to look out, and there's a lot to do, getting Gran's things sorted ready for the carrier. But I'd love to come again to see you — and Miss Agatha too — before I go. Goodbye, then, Miss Mildred."

Feeling rather like Alice emerging from Wonderland, I set off for home.

13

It was true. At a point about half way along the side of the toolshed, someone had been digging. The turned soil had dried out, but it still appeared fresh.

I stood looking at it, while the recent words of the ladies at Witches' Corner ran a chilly finger up my spine. Ghosts, spirits, darkness and shifting lights, digging . . . The word they combined to suggest was *grave*. Even on that sunny day the word was cold.

Then I took a pull at myself. A grave? The disturbed patch of earth was roughly two feet square, no more. If something really was buried here, it could not be anything much bigger than a cat.

Buried. This time the word held none of the chilling connotations of "digging". The word that went with it was "treasure". People buried treasure. And a treasure of a kind had been stolen. I could think of no reason at all why anyone should rob

Gran's safe and then bury the proceeds a few yards away in the garden, but I had to find out if that was what had happened.

And of course I had no spade. Davey, as I was being reminded with tiresome frequency, had all the tools. But this time I was not prepared to wait till he came by, or to go up to the Hall for him. There ought to be a shovel in the coal-house. Awkward and heavy, but it would have to do.

I went to get it, half expecting to find that it, too, had gone with the rest. But no, it was there, propped just inside the coal-house door. I hefted it to one shoulder and went back to the shed. As I poised the shovel for the first stroke I noticed two things; there was dried earth on it, mixed with the residue of coal dust, and now that I looked, there were traces of coal dust in the soil of the "grave".

So Miss Mildred's intruder, whoever he was, had had to use the coal-shovel, too. She had seen the light on Monday, and the tools had been taken the previous week. It fitted. She could be right. I dug.

I dug for twenty back-breaking minutes.

That wretched shovel got me down to nearly one and a half feet, and then I struck undisturbed clay. And nothing else. Nothing was buried there.

So the hunt was still on for the missing treasures. I put the shovel away and went in to wash and make myself some lunch.

At least there was no difficulty about finding the photograph album. There had never been many books at Rose Cottage; Gran read weekly magazines, which she called "books", and very little else, except the Bible. This lived in the bottom drawer of the sideboard, and the album was there with it. It was more than an album, it was a sort of family record book; besides the photographs there was an envelope full of old, yellowed news-clippings, mostly, as I saw at a quick glance, about prizes Granddad had taken at flower shows, or cuttings from the local paper about the doings of the family at the Hall. About my mother's flight from home, or about her death, there was nothing. Either she was not news enough even for the *Echo,* or my grandmother had not cared to keep the record. I found ballpoint and writing-pad, and sat down to make the list of dates the vicar wanted.

I doubt if it would be possible for any-one, who has not seen it for some years, to work quickly through an old family al-bum. It took me well into the afternoon to find all the relevant dates, then, after a pause for a cup of tea, I turned to Gran's list, and busied myself with looking out the small things she wanted, and ranging them, ready for packing, on the sideboard or the table in the back kitchen.

The evening was shading to dusk, and I had finished my supper and got the dishes washed and put away, when there was a soft rapping at the door. Wondering who could have come here at this hour, I went to open it, to find Miss Linsey out-side. The light from the window, outlining her against the growing dusk, made her look almost ghostly. She had on some kind of cloak, grey and shapeless, which she clutched to her, and above it her hair looked wilder than ever.

She spoke in a whisper, with a glance over her shoulder so nervously furtive that I found myself looking about to see if anyone else was lurking near. But garden and lane were empty.

"It's only me, Kathy, May I come in?"

"Well, of course. How nice to see you again, Miss Linsey." I stood back, holding the door for her. "I'm afraid I haven't lighted the fire, but please —"

"No matter, no matter." She slid, rather than walked past me as she spoke.

"Will you let me take your cloak, or would you rather keep it?"

The polite commonplaces didn't seem to have the desired effect, of taking out whatever drama she saw in the situation. She went into the kitchen in a kind of breathless rush, looking to see that I had shut the door safely behind her. Then, still clutching the cloak round her, she rotated slowly, as if to check that no one besides ourselves was there in the little room.

"Your door wasn't locked." The whisper was a little stronger, but it was still a whisper.

"Well, no. We never used to lock it. Have things changed hereabouts?" I smiled, trying to give the reassurance she seemed to need. It was difficult not to whisper back. "I did ask the vicar if the gipsies had been here again, but he says there's been no sign of them. And even when they were here —"

"That's it. That's just it. They have been back."

I was reaching up to the mantelpiece for a match to put to the fire. I stopped in mid-action and turned. She nodded, with a glance to left and right, and I thought her eyes looked not so much mad as distressed.

"Just let me get the fire going," I said, "and sit here in the rocking-chair. That's it. It'll soon be warm, and then we can talk."

The fire, which I had relaid after a fashion, caught, flickered, then burned up into a cheerful blaze. Miss Linsey subsided into Gran's chair, let her cloak slip back, and spread her hands out to the warmth.

"You'll take a cup of tea." I didn't wait for an answer, but went to fill the kettle. When I returned with the tray bearing the tea-things I found that she had the album on her knee, and was slowly turning the pages.

I set the tray down. "Milk and sugar?"

"No sugar, thank you." Then as I put the cup on the oven-top beside her she said, on a faint note like a sigh, "Ah. Yes. It was. I knew it."

I looked at the open page on her knee. It held four small photographs, in faded black and white. They had been taken, I knew, with the cheap little box Brownie camera that Granddad had treasured. The prints were not more than two-and-a-half by one-and-a-half inches, but the focus was sharp, and the detail pretty good. There was one of Gran sitting outside the cottage door, with her lace-pillow on her knee. I remembered how years ago she had made the delicate lace to sell. Another of her down near the gate, picking beans, and with her myself, a very small girl, bare-footed, in a print dress with a cotton bonnet on my head, and a basket for the beans held in both hands. One of me on the step of the front porch with my arms round the neck of our old dog, Nip. The fourth was a delightful snap, taking in a lucky moment, of a slender, lovely girl, standing just inside the garden gate with an armful of flowers. She was laughing. In my memory, except when I had last seen her, she was always laughing. My mother, Lilias.

"They're good, aren't they?" I made my voice as prosaic as possible. "I was just checking some dates. The album's a bit heavy, isn't it? Let me."

I took it from her and put it back on the table, then sat down on the opposite side of the fire.

Before I could speak again she leaned forward, the eyes fixed again, intense. "You would hardly remember her, I suppose. How old were you when she left? Five? Six? But I knew her well. And she wasn't someone you could forget very easily, she was such a pretty creature. So very pretty. Poor girl. If only I had known in those days when I know now, I could have warned her . . . But then it would have been so different, wouldn't it?"

"I suppose it would. But Miss Linsey, you were saying that the gypsies had been back. Did Miss Mildred tell you what she told me this afternoon?"

"Not if it was anything important," she said, sounding all at once surprisingly normal. "She never does. I think Sister" — the word came out in a fair imitation of Miss Mildred's slightly tremulous falsetto — "warns her that I'm not reliable, because she can only see what's there in front of her eyes, and Millie can't even see that. She's a dear creature, but very unworldly, of course." She sipped tea. "Do you know, I don't think she even knows what the bees are doing to her precious flowers?"

I laughed. "Henry?"

"Yes. She spent half an hour this morning trying to persuade me to hatch that wretched egg, even when I told her that I'd had Henry here alone in my garden for three years. But she's such a dear, and at least she doesn't try to put one *down* the way Agatha does."

Remembering Miss Agatha, I knew what she meant. That efficient business lady would have no patience with what she had called (according to Gran) "airy-fairy goings-on, and why doesn't she set up as a fortune-teller and make a little money with a crystal ball or some such rubbish, instead of living on bread and greens and whatever my soft-hearted little sister gives her?"

She put her cup aside, settling back comfortably into the folds of her wrap. The hunted look had gone, but she still looked troubled. "I'm sorry to disturb you so late, Kathy, but I couldn't really get away till now without Millie seeing me, and I thought she might try to stop me. You saw what happened this morning. I did try to tell you then, but there was all the fuss about Henry, and to be honest, I think dear Millie changed the subject deliberately."

"She may have done, but she had just told me something herself, and I think she may have been afraid of making me nervous. You said you'd had a dream about my mother, and about the gipsy she ran off with." I showed a hand. "It's all right, it's a long time ago, and everyone knows the story. It's all over, and nothing to do with me now."

"But that's just it. It's not all over. It started with something I saw. It may have been a dream, I don't know. I did see her, and the gipsy with her. They had a light, a lantern, and they were in the lonnen, where that old caravan is — you know the one I mean?"

"Yes, but Miss Linsey — no, please listen! I know you have the Sight, and I do believe that you see things that other people can't, and that you dream things and then they come true. I remember what Gran told me about it, and when I was little we all knew." I tried a smile. "We were a bit afraid of you. We thought you might be a witch. But this about seeing my mother — she's dead, and Jamie — that was the gipsy's name — is dead, too. And that old caravan, well, if it is still there, it'll have dropped to pieces by this time. What would anyone go there for?" I added, gently, "It must have been a dream, Miss Linsey."

"But there was a light. I saw a light."

"There was someone down here the other night with a light. That's what Miss Mildred told me this afternoon. Monday night. She thought she saw someone out there by the toolshed, and when I got home I looked around, and it's true that someone has been there, digging, but I can't think why. There's nothing there."

"That would be Davey Pascoe." She spoke impatiently. "He took the tools. That's nothing to do with it. And it wasn't Monday when I saw them, Lilias and her gipsy. I know it wasn't Monday. And I didn't say they were down here at the cottage."

She turned that light, bright gaze on me again, but I had the uncomfortable feeling that she was not seeing me. "The caravan — perhaps you are right about that. That was a different time and yes, now that I remember it, the lantern shone through the trees, and the caravan wasn't broken at all, and there was a horse grazing, and she came running up the lonnen with a bag in each hand —"

"Miss Linsey —" I spoke breathlessly, but she took no notice. She swept on, still looking past me as if the cottage walls had melted into the dusk.

"And then they weren't there. They weren't there. That's right. That was a dream. Mildred's wrong. They were in the lonnen, not at the cottage."

I said nothing. A coal fell in the grate, and the little noise seemed to bring her back, and to rebuild the firelit room round us. She turned to me.

"But the other time wasn't the same. They were in the cemetery. And they didn't have a lantern then. He had a torch, an ordinary electric torch. He was shining it down on the grave."

That frisson again at the word. I didn't speak. Her eyes focused on me, disturbed and disturbing still, but not mad. Certainly not mad.

She gave a nod. "You do understand. It isn't always easy to keep the two kinds of reality apart. So please forgive me, and forget it if you can, the dream about the caravan. Even if it happened like that, it was a long time ago."

"I know."

She set her tea-cup aside and leaned forward. She had abandoned her whispering, and the normal, everyday tones somehow helped to enforce belief, as if she really had come out of her dream-country to the reality of every day.

"But this was real, Kathy, and it happened on Sunday. I do always go to the cemetery on a Sunday, after the evening service, to tend Albert's grave — my brother, you never knew him — and Mrs Winton Smith had kept me talking, something about the Sunday School Treat, where I always help, so I was late, and when I got to the cemetery it was dark, but the light from the torch was reflected from a white headstone, that marble angel with the Bible, and I recognised her."

"But Miss Linsey, please! I'm not sure — are you really trying to tell me — what are you trying to tell me? That you think you saw —" I hesitated. "I don't know what you think you saw. But in any case it's nearly twenty years —"

"I know." Still that practical, everyday tone of voice. "That's why I said she was carrying her age well. Still so lovely, and in that light . . . I suppose my vision of her at the caravan — call it a dream if you find that a more comfortable word — my dream had reminded me of what she was like, but I was sure."

"I —" I took a deep breath. I found my heart had quickened uncomfortably, and I had to make an effort to keep the disbelieving protest out of my voice. "Look, Miss Linsey, all right. But if you were so sure it was, yes, let's put into words — if you were so sure it was my mother, still alive and back here in Todhall, why didn't you *say* something? Call out, or go closer and speak to her — at least ask her what had happened and what she was doing there?"

"I tried to," she said simply. "I did say something, and I tried to hurry, but I tripped over a kerbstone and dropped my flowers, and when I got up they were gone."

" 'They'? You said 'they'. Who was with her?"

"I couldn't see him very well, and of course I never knew him, but he was tall and dark, like the gipsy, the one at the caravan."

"And when you tried to speak or approach them, they disappeared? Just vanished?"

She nodded, but as if answering a question I had not asked. "Yes, I know, my dear. You're kind, and you have good manners, and you listen, but you still don't believe. Well, I don't understand it any more than you do, and perhaps I was mistaken, but I had to tell you. I do believe that I saw them there, both together, on Sunday, by the grave."

"By your brother's grave?" I said, blankly.

"Oh, no! What would they be doing there? It was your Aunt Betsy's."

She went soon after that, refusing my offer to see her as far as the road. She had never been afraid of the dark, she told me, with something of a return to her earlier manner; night was more interesting than day. On this note she floated off, a shapeless ghost muffled in cloak and scarf, to vanish into the shadows of the lane.

Interesting indeed. I retreated rather smartly into the comforting firelight of the cottage kitchen, trying to think sensibly and coolly about what she had told me. It could not be true. It obviously could not be true. But, perhaps illogically, the very fact that her vision of the young Lilias's flight into the lonnen was apparently so accurate, bade one believe that her tale of the couple in the cemetery might be true, even if her interpretation of it was not.

I added the album to the goods laid ready for packing, then rummaged in the drawer for an envelope, ready for the list of dates for the vicar that would go up with the milk in the morning. As I folded the notes and sealed the envelope my mind raced away again, putting together the odd things that had happened. The light in the cottage garden. The empty safe — robbed by someone who had a key. The digging by the toolshed. And now this weird and unlikely story of Lilias and her gipsy at Aunt Betsy's grave-side . . .

Comfortingly, none of it added up to anything believable. Lilias back from the dead, and Not getting in touch with Gran or myself? not going near anyone in the village? Coming back from a long silence of some sixteen years, during which time neither her mother nor her daughter had had a word from her? Coming back, apparently, simply to visit the grave of the woman she had, with reason, hated, and then vanishing like a ghost at Miss Linsey's approach?

I got briskly to my feet, propped the envelope behind the empty milk-bottle in the porch, along with a biscuit for Rosy, then I raked out the remains of the fire, and locked both doors before going up to bed.

I didn't want any more of Miss Linsey's interesting things to happen while I was alone at Rose Cottage.

14

I was awakened next morning by the sound of Rosy's hoofs in the lane. I had not found it easy to get to sleep. The night had been quite silent and uneventful, but I kept thinking about Miss Linsey's ghosts. If Miss Mildred's story of the light at the cottage, and the digging, was true — as seemed to be proved by the disturbed patch near the toolshed and the state of the coal-shovel — then it was possible, just possible, that Miss Linsey's story of the couple with the light at the site of the old caravan might have some truth in it as well. As for her "seeing" of the young Lilias running up the lonnen with a bag in either hand, that was a story known by this time to everyone in the village, and she had admitted it to be merely a dream, but I was well aware that she had not been called a witch for nothing. I could think of at least two occasions when her prophetic "dream" of a disaster

had been right, and on one of those occasions a life had been saved. So it might
at least be worth looking into.

But her story of the couple encountered
in the cemetery was harder to explain. Her
Sunday evening visit to her brother's grave
must have been real enough, but the en-
counter with the ghostly couple was surely
a trick of the imagination, suggested, perhaps, by the other dream? For Miss Linsey
to recognnise Lilias, a Lilias last seen almost twenty years ago, and now glimpsed
at some distance in the evening dusk, and
then to have her and her gipsy companion
vanish when approached — it had to be a
dream, and dreams, as all Todhall knew,
were Miss Linsey's stock-in-trade.

But what had so disturbed me about it
was the fact that she had not enjoyed telling me. Had been, if not frightened, then
deeply uneasy. So could there be some
sort of "message" here for me? Some sort
of ghostly getting-in-touch, like those
prophecies of hers that the village still remembered with respect?

Which was nonsense, I told myself.
And maybe I had missed a chance to
solve my own mystery. With Miss Linsey

in soothsaying mood, I should have asked her where Gran's treasures had vanished to . . .

On which robust note I turned over and went to sleep, and woke to the sound of the milk-cart and the creak of the garden gate.

I flung back the bedclothes and ran to the open casement.

"Good morning, Mr Blaney! I'm sorry, I slept in. Just a pint, please, and I wonder if you'd be good enough to leave that envelope at the vicarage? The vicar's expecting it."

"That's all right. No bother at all. Lovely day, isn't it? You staying on till the weekend? Well, don't you trouble yourself, you just get your sleep, and I'll leave you one tomorrow, and it'll be two on Saturday. We don't do a round on a Sunday."

I noticed the "we". Sunday wouldn't be his day off, farmers didn't have them. It was Rosy's. I had forgotten that. I smiled. "Yes, thank you. It looks as if I'm to be here at least till Monday. And that's Rosy's biscuit under the envelope."

He took it, pocketed the envelope,

waved the empty bottle in salute, and went off.

Somehow his simple kindness made the worries of the night seem trivial. Cheered and soothed, I dressed and had breakfast and then, after finishing the morning's chores, went out to gather flowers for Granddad's grave. That I chose to visit the cemetery this morning was, I told myself, nothing to do with Miss Linsey's story. I had intended to go one day while I was here, to take flowers on Gran's behalf and for myself, and to check, as she had asked me to, that the sexton was earning the small fee he got for keeping the grave-plot tidy.

That was all. Nothing to do with ghosts, or a witch's dreams.

I didn't bother to find an excuse for what I did after I had gathered the flowers and packed them carefully with some damp moss into a basket. The cemetery lay at the south end of the village, and the short-est way would of course have been by the lane. The other route was by the lonnen, which reached the main road a good quar-ter of a mile beyond the cemetery wall.

I went by the lonnen.

* * *

There was a stronger breeze today, and the birds were still busy with their morning songs. Deep in the lane the air was still, full of the scents of fern and dead leaves and wild garlic and the musk of Herb Robert trodden underfoot. High overhead the treetops rustled and soughed, but where I walked it was like being at the bottom of a deep, still stream. The only movement was the sudden whisk of russet-brown as a squirrel scudded up a tree-trunk, and the flight of a blackbird cutting low across the path with a beakful of food for its young.

The remains of the caravan were still there, some little way about the gap where I had entered the lonnen on my way from the station. Elder and brambles were growing round and into it, and everywhere there were nettles, those jackal plants that follow humans and take over their deserted homes.

One wheel lay flat, barely visible in long grass. The other was still held, at a crazy slant, by a rusted bolt. The wood of both was almost rotted away, held only by the decaying iron rims. The van itself was a rotten shell, its roof fallen in and its sides sagging. The shafts, the whole front rig, had come adrift and was in pieces on the ground.

It was a long-forgotten wreck which could not possibly have anything to tell me. Nevertheless I set my basket down and prodded about among the crumbling wood and the undergrowth, picking up a few nettle-stings and a scratch or two from the brambles, but no message from the past. Nothing left by the ghosts of Miss Linsey's vision. Just a host of memories, my own ghosts, remembered with amusement and a kind of sadness, the ghosts of the children who had played in this lane, and for whom this derelict gipsy-van had been at once romantic and terrifying, and a goal of challenge and delight.

A sound brought me round, my heart suddenly thudding, as if the place had not wholly lost its terror. A sound which in any other place would hardly even have made me turn my head. A breaking twig, and the slither of a footstep on the bank above me.

The sun, blazing through a gap at the

top of the bank, was blinding me. Against it, at the head of the bank, stood a man, gigantic against the distorting brilliance, body bent forward to stare down at me. He grabbed a branch, swung himself through the gap, and came down the bank at a run, and it was only Davey Pascoe, in his working overalls, and not looking in the least like the menacing gipsy giant that my nerves had conjured up. In fact, so wrapped had I been in my memories that it came as a kind of shock to see him there, a young man with the same thatch of light-brown hair and the same grey eyes as the child whose ghost, a moment before, had been playing there.

I let my breath out. "Damn you, Davey! You frightened me!"

"Did I? Well, you disappointed me. I heard something moving about down here, and I thought it might be a badger. There's a sett further up, and they do sometimes come out in daylight."

"Really. Well, I'm sorry. But what were you doing here anyway?"

"I've been at Swords. The job's finished, so I thought I'd come back this way and see how you were getting on. I'm not working this afternoon, and I thought you might be starting to sort the stuff out for packing."

"Well, thanks, but I haven't done much yet." I indicated the basket of flowers. "I was going to the cemetery with those."

"Why this way? It's quicker by the lane." He grinned, and it was the grin I remembered. "Or did someone dare you?"

"Who'd do that? I never took the dare anyway. No, I came because I wanted to see —" I stopped. I was not sure myself just what I had wanted to see.

"See what?"

"I don't know. It sounds silly. The van, I suppose. I've wondered, sometimes, if there's any way you could tell where it was made or who owned it. You know, like a number plate on a car."

"After all this time? Even if there was, it's gone long since." He was frowning now. "Look, Kathy, it's past history. You'll do yourself no good by trying to rake it all up again now. Can't you let yourself see that it's past?" He finished it deliberately. "Past and dead and gone."

The three syllables fell like stones. I turned and picked up the basket.

"Yes. I know. I've accepted that long ago. I've had to. Don't worry about me, Davey. I don't want to rake anything up that's better left alone. But we've got this mystery on our hands, Gran's things being stolen, and I thought — well, something happened last night that set me wondering, and I came along here to check it out."

"Last night?" he said sharply. "What happened? Has anyone been bothering you at the cottage?"

"No, no. Nothing like that. It was Miss Linsey. She came to see me, and told me some very queer things."

He laughed. "Old Linsey-woolsey? I'll bet. Such as?"

"Oh, it's a long story, and it'll sound queerer still in daylight?"

"Well, queer or not, I'll listen. Here, give me that basket. I'll go back with you, and you can tell me about it."

His bicycle was at the head of the bank, propped against a stump. He slung the basket over the handlebars and, as we walked up through the field towards the road, with Davey wheeling the bicycle, I told him about Miss Linsey's visit.

His reaction was, I suppose, predictable.

"Silly old bat, saying she didn't want to scare you, and then doing her best to give you nightmares! Well, you can forget all that about your mum running up the lonnen. I could've said all that to you myself, there's no one in the village that hadn't heard all about her taking off like that, and, I might say," he added, "there's no one who blames her, running away from that old catamaran — well, speak no ill, and there's two sides to everything. But this tale of old Linsey-woolsey's about the couple at the graveside — that might be interesting, seeing what else has happened. I mean, there's been someone at the cottage, that's for sure, and it might just be that — Oh, well, leave it for now. Here we are, and we can go in by the side gate. Your Granda's near it, you'll remember, a little way along."

There was a door set into the high brick wall of the cemetery. Davey leaned the bicycle there, retrieved my basket for me, and pushed open the door.

15

The cemetery was large — two fields taken over from Low Beck Farm when the old churchyard became too crowded to be serviceable — and surrounded by a high wall. My grandfather's grave was about midway along the west side, a large plot, to leave space, as I remembered Gran saying, for late-comers. Among the flowers I had brought for him were clusters of his favourite rose, the cottage rose, Old Blush, which he had planted in every available space at home, because, he said, they wouldn't let him grow "the real roses" at the Hall, just "those coloured cabbages they breed nowadays, all size and no scent".

"You'll want water for those," said Davey. "The tap's over near the main gate, and there's usually a can there. I'll get it for you." He went off, leaving me to go to the grave-side alone.

I had stopped to set my basket down at

the kerbside before I realised that, when I
had gathered the flowers that morning, I
had not even thought about taking any for
Aunt Betsy. Admittedly, she had never ex-
pressed a preference for, or even an opin-
ion of, any flower or plant, except to
complain about the scent of the wild garlic
in the lane, but even so —

I need not have troubled. On the grave-
space next to my grandfather's there were
already flowers, masses of them, arranged
with some care in a couple of metal urns.
Not roses, but a mixture of garden and
wild flowers, lupins and delphiniums and
Canterbury bells, along with dog-daisies
and cornflowers, and trails of ivy and wild
honeysuckle. The wild flowers were all
dead or dying, but the others were fresh
still.

Even in the presence of the quiet dead
it is not easy to control one's thoughts.
My first one was, who in the world would
have done this for that very unpopular old
woman, my great-aunt? My second was
that she herself would have called it a sin-
ful waste, and Popish at that.

So who? Miss Linsey's ghosts? My
dead mother and her long-dead gipsy,

creeping after dark into the cemetery with this charming tribute to someone whom, in life, she had disliked, even hated, whose viper's tongue had driven her from home? If there was any sort of truth in Miss Linsey's tale of lights and people at the grave, no ghosts had put these flowers there. Then who? Not Gran; she had known that I would visit the grave-plot, and she surely would have told me if she had asked anyone else to bring flowers.

A sudden breeze stirred the grasses by the wall, sending a couple of petals floating to the ground, and bringing with it the scent of roses, and with the scent, a vivid memory of a garden crammed with roses and lupins and all the flowers of summer. Miss Mildred's garden. Miss Mildred, the one person I knew whose simple loving-kindness would have embraced even Aunt Betsy. Whose loving-kindness put me to shame.

I detached a sprig of the cottage rose from the bunch in my basket, and laid it on her grave, then turned to give the rest to Granddad.

He, too, had been visited. In the vase near the headstone was a bunch of roses, chief among them the silvery pink of his beloved Old Blush.

"Who in the world?" I asked. "Miss Mildred?"

"Might be," said Davey. He had returned with a can of water, and we had puzzled over it together. There was no card or message. "But I've not seen flowers here before. Well, we can ask her, but I doubt it's not her."

Another "we", and in its own way as comforting as Mr Blaney's. I smiled at him, and knelt to replace the fading roses in the vase with the fresh ones I had brought. "Then who?"

"Dear knows, but you see what it might mean? Look at those flowers. The garden ones are still okay, but the wild ones, the cornflowers and such, they're all dead. Which they would be, if they've been there since Sunday."

I sat back on my heels, staring up at him. "Then you really think that? Miss Linsey's ghosts?"

"I reckon so. Who else? It fits. Somebody brought them. Somebody's been here. It could be folk your aunt had known at home in Scotland, maybe, visiting nearby, and they came over, and old Linsey-woolsey saw them."

"But Davey, they vanished. She said they just disappeared."

He pointed to the door we had come in by. "She'd have come in by the main gate. If her two ghosts came in the way we did and left the door open, it's only a couple of steps out to the road, and they'd gone. It was pretty dark Sunday night."

"Ye-es. Yes, you could be right. But who? And if it was friends of the family, Gran's family, why didn't they go into the village, to see your mother, perhaps? Or to Rose Cottage —" I stopped.

"Yeah," said Davey. "That's what it comes to, isn't it? They did go to Rose Cottage. They may have come to see Mum as well, but there was nobody home at our place last weekend. Look, let's not worry about it now. If they came to leave flowers here, they mean no harm to you and yours, that's for sure. And if you're thinking what I think you are, stop it."

"I — I don't know what to think."

"Then don't try. Have you finished your flowers?"

"Yes." I stood up, watching while he tilted the can to trickle water into the vases. "Look, why don't we stop by Witches' Corner and ask Miss Mildred if she brought the flowers. Get that bit clear, at least."

"No good. She's not home. She went into Sunderland this morning, and it's my guess the two of them'll go to the pictures and get home late. There, I needn't have bothered to get the water. There's plenty. Hang on while I tip the rest out. Those pansies could do with a drop, and that rose bush by the wall. That's it. Okay. Tell you what, we'll go home, and Mum'll give us some dinner, and maybe talk some sense into us."

As it happened, Mrs Pascoe did not get the chance, as, by unspoken consent, neither Davey nor I mentioned Miss Linsey or the riddle of the cemetery. We told her merely that we had met in Gipsy Lonnen, and that he had gone back with me to put flowers on the graves, and brought me home for dinner.

"If that's all right?" I said. An unexpected guest could pose problems with food rationing.

"Lord bless you, child, of course it is. There's plenty, and you're welcome. Davey, get her a knife and fork, and go and call your father."

She refused my offer of help, told me briskly to sit down, and began to dish up a large chicken pie. "And had old Tom been doing a good job on the graves?"

"Mr Corner told me he was still sexton, and I could hardly believe it! Does he do it all himself still? I used to think he was about a hundred, and that's years ago."

"Eighty-two, and won't even talk about retiring. He does get help with the grave-digging, though."

"Well, the place was very tidy, and the grave looked fine." I hesitated, then asked her merely if Miss Mildred was in the habit of taking flowers to the cemetery. She knew nothing about that, she said, with a kind of snort, but she did know that poor Miss Mildred wasn't even welcome, these days, to take them to the church, since the vicar's wife fancied her own stuff so much, and looked down her nose at other people's.

"And now there's none coming in from the Hall — here, Jim," as Mr Pascoe and Davey came in, "yours is ready." She set his plate down, and spooned potatoes. "Have you washed your hands, Davey?"

"Yes, Mum," said Davey, and winked at me as he took his place.

Mr Pascoe greeted me as he sat down. He was a quiet, mild-mannered man, who was known for miles around as an excellent craftsman. He was, in looks, an older version of Davey; an inch or so shorter, perhaps, and with the thicker body and greying hair of middle age, but the same grey eyes and indefinable poise of self-belief that marks the man who knows his limitations, but who also knows what he is good for, and expects — and receives — the respect it brings him. It was a dignity which, I supposed, carried over from the other part of his profession. He was, of course, the local undertaker.

"Davey says you've been to see the graves? They'd be all right, old Tom does the grass every Friday, rain or shine. By the way, Kathy, I've been on to Caslaws, and they'll do your move for you Monday at latest, but there's a chance of Saturday, so you'd best be ready. Davey can take time off to give you a hand."

"Thank you very much."

"You're welcome, you know that. Give the girl some more of those potatoes, Mother. She'll be on short rations down there at the cottage."

"No, really, I've got plenty. The pie's lovely, Aunty Annie."

Mrs Pascoe primmed her lips, looking pleased. "Well, eat up," she said, and sitting down she began to ask me about the Brandons and Gran's new house, while Davey and his father ate busily and, when they spoke at all, exchanged brief comments about the work they were doing at the Hall.

I helped clear the plates, and while Mrs Pascoe was dishing the pudding — a hearty syrup sponge — I asked her, "Was there much damage done at the Hall in the war? Gran said it was a mess, though I suppose you can't blame the boys. The RAF, I mean."

She gave me a quick, sideways look.

"Nobody blames them, poor lads. We all know what they did for us, and if that's any comfort to you, it's the truth."

"Thank you. These two plates for the men?"

"That one was for you. If it's too much, give it to Davey. No, the Hall wasn't too bad, really, just scratches and chips everywhere, and the floors a bit of a mess. Nothing that can't be repaired, with a bit of plaster and a lick of paint and some polish to bring it up lovely again. No real harm done. We'd moved some of the breakables down to the cellar, and the carpets from the drawing-room, and the pictures, and things like that. The books are still down there."

"Is the kitchen still the same?"

"The big kitchen, yes. They put a modern stove in the servery, and the cooking was mostly done there. The library's the worst. That's where the bar was."

"I can imagine."

She primmed her mouth again, but looked amused. "Well, they had a dartboard there. Where old Sir Giles's portrait used to be."

"Oh dear."

"But the billiard room's all right. Some-one must have kept their eye on that."

"Billiard room?" said Davey. "You talking about Toad Hall?"

Mrs Pascoe tut-tutted, and I laughed as I got up to help her with the dishes. I had forgotten the name which, inevitably, had stuck to Tod Hall once *The Wind in the Willows* reached our classroom. Our eld-ers, afraid of the Hall's reaction, had tried, but in vain, to stop us using it.

"I'm taking the van across this after-noon," said Davey, to me. "Want to come over with me?"

"I thought you said you weren't working this afternoon?"

"I'm not. But Dad wants some tools bringing that he left there, and there's some timber needs carting over as well. Wouldn't you like to see the place?"

"Well, yes, I would. I'll be writing to Gran tonight, and I know she'd like to hear what's going on."

"If you're writing to your Gran —" said Mr Pascoe. "Annie, lass, there's that pa-per the masons sent. Can you think on where we put it?"

"It's behind the clock on the mantel-piece. Get it for your Dad, Davey."

"Give it to Kathy," said Mr Pascoe. "There you are, Kathy, maybe you'll send it to your Gran, if you're writing. I'd have asked her about it myself, if she'd been on the phone. They want to know about the text for the stone."

"The stone?"

"Your Aunt Betsy's headstone. Well, it's the same stone, of course, your Grand-dad's. There's space left, as you know. The masons have taken long enough, they always do, but I wrote a while ago to ask them what was keeping them back, and they said they were still waiting for the text. You know how most folk like some-thing from the Bible put on the stone, and your Gran did say something about it, but I reckon she's forgotten."

"Well, I'll ask her, but she probably didn't want one." I thought of the Unseen Guest, who would have been welcome, I was sure, in this kindly house. "I think she had enough of them at home. But I'll ask her, certainly."

"And tell her we were asking after her."

This, being translated, was "give her our

love". I promised, smiling, and was inter-rupted by Davey, sounding impatient.

"Are you coming? If we go now I can get you back in plenty of time for your date with the vicar."

I glanced at Mrs Pascoe as I hung the tea-towel to dry above the fireplace.

"You go on," she said. "I'll be quicker putting the things away myself. I know where they go."

As she turned to stack the clean dishes away in a cupboard, I thought she was smiling.

16

Davey drove the van round to the back of the Hall, and under the archway into the courtyard. This was a wide, cobbled square, with the old mounting-block at its centre, and on two sides the stable doors and the archways of the coach-house. One of the other sides had held offices and quarters — now mostly storerooms — for those servants who had lived in, and on the fourth side were the back premises of the Hall itself.

I remembered the courtyard as a peaceful place, where doves strutted and cooed, or flew up in mock alarm when the stable clock struck or a gardener wheeled his barrow across the cobbles. But today it was very different. Evidences of the proposed conversion were everywhere, piles of bricks, a cement-mixer, ladders, buckets, timber, and an unattractive collection of bathroom fittings still pasted up with strips of gummed wrapping. And there was something else that was new, or rather, unexpected after the gap of years. The smell of horses. The stable half-doors and the old tack-room door stood open, and outside was a pile of manure sweepings ready to be carted off, presumably, to the garden heap.

"Horses?" I said to Davey. "Who's got horses here now?"

"It's a riding-school, has been for nearly two years now, and the family thought it'd be a good idea to having riding here for the hotel. You remember Harry Coleman?"

I remembered Harry Coleman, a good-looking boy a couple of years older than myself, who had been in the senior class at school. For one long blushful year I had been one of his worshipping admirers. One of the crowd. He went up to the secondary school two years before me, and was there, ready to receive our homage once more, when Prissy and I were enrolled. He was kind to us, unbending from the height of his achievements in the sports field, and our greatest privilege had been to travel back to Todhall with him in the same carriage, and carry his school bag to his home gate. Luckily his home gate had been very near the station. His father farmed Low Beck, which belonged to the Hall.

"Handsome Harry?" I said. "Running a riding place here?"

"Aye. Doesn't make much out of that yet. The schoolteacher goes there, and a couple of boys from Fishburn way, but he keeps horses there, at livery he calls it, for some of the locals — Mr Taylor's got one, and Jim Sands, and the Blake girl from Deepings. They hunt with the South Durham. It was Harry thought of it, and his Dad put the cash up, so the family let them have the stables. They reckon it'll be an extra draw once the hotel gets going."

"I remember Harry was always keen, and his father kept a good horse for him. I was there when he won the cup at Sedgefield. He used to talk about Olympia, but of course there was the war. Did he ever get there?"

"Not that I ever heard, and if he had we'd have all heard," said Davey drily. He swung down from the cab and turned to unlash the timber from the roof of the van. "I'll get this stuff stacked in the coach-house under cover. D'you want to go into the house now? Here's the key."

"Yes, I'd like to. How long will you be?"

"Not long, but there's no hurry. I'll come and fetch you."

He shouldered some of the timber and tramped off towards one of the coach-house archways. I made for the back door. It opened on a long passage floored with stone flags. There was evidence here, too, that work was being done, but when I reached the kitchen I found it much the same as I remembered it.

For a house built in the early nineteenth century, the kitchen was a good one. It was on ground level, and the big, barred windows, though they faced north, looked out over the walled kitchen-garden. There were few concessions to modern living, so I supposed it was inevitable that, to make it viable as a hotel kitchen, the working premises would have to be stripped and totally rebuilt.

Why was it that one always regretted change? Things were not made to stay fixed, preserved in amber. Perhaps the only acceptable amber was memory. I had "helped" in this kitchen so many times. I could remember when the table-tops were above my eye-level, and I shared the floor under the table with the dog, waiting, both of us, for the piece of cake or biscuit to be handed down and shared. The kitchen, the heart of the house, with its warmth and its wonderful smells of baking, or the delectable smell of roasting meat, and the sizzle and spit as the joint was speared and turned in the pan. The clashing of pots and dishes and the cheerful chatter of women's voices. A whole world, once. And now changed, and soon to be changed again. And, surely, for the better? One had to believe that the world was changing for the better, or else why live? That, arguably, was one of the facets of what Christians called faith?

I left the empty kitchen and once again went through the green baize door that shut the servants' quarters off from the main house. That first door led to the dining-room, where sometimes I had helped Alice, the parlourmaid, to set the table.

The big room was empty now, echoing, stripped and waiting for the contractors.

No stab of regret here, no memories. I shut the door on it and went along to the hall. This — the great hall, as we called it — was a room in itself. The front door opened into it, and there was a huge open fireplace to one side, usually protected by screens from the draughts that were everywhere. The main staircase was opposite the door, a wide flight rising to a landing, where it divided, the twin stairs leading to the two wings of the house. The landing was lit, grudgingly, by a stained-glass window. The only time, Gran had said, that the hall had been habitable — in fact the only time I had ever been in it — was at Christmas, when we schoolchildren had come carol-singing with the vicar, and there had been a fire in the vast fireplace, and a tree, and a mince pie and an orange for each child.

The drawing-room lay on the south side of the hall. The big double doors were shut. I hesitated for a moment, then, feeling as guilty as if I were invading Bluebeard's chamber, I pushed them open.

A blaze of light met me, from three big

floor-length windows that threw sharp patterns of sunshine slanting across an acre or so of unpolished parquet floor. A pair of Chinese carpets, presumably restored from their place in the cellars, lay in front of the twin fireplaces, with chairs and sofas disposed here and there. There was a grand piano, covered and, it was to be hoped, undamaged. A writing desk. A big breakfront bookcase, empty of books. Not much else in the way of furniture, but pictures, lamps, and a couple of vast Chinese jars on carved pedestals, all back in place. It was a beautiful room still, a room that looked as if it had only been temporarily abandoned, and could be lived in, and loved, again. Even its owners were still there; above the fireplaces hung the portraits — done presumably soon after they took over the Hall — of Sir James and Lady Brandon.

I stood looking up at the portrait of the young Sir James.

Immaculate in riding clothes, he was pictured with horse and dogs beside a tree in the park, but, I thought, put him in uniform and make him smile, and he could have sat for the photograph of his son Gilbert that I had seen in Lady Brandon's sitting-room at Strathbeg. It was the same boy, dark-haired, dark-eyed, and handsome . . .

"Changed a bit, hasn't he?" asked Davey, behind me.

"Well, don't we all? You have."

"And you," said Davey.

"Yes. Well, it's been a long time." I turned away towards a window. "I was just thinking how like him Gilbert was. Not that I saw him after he'd gone away to school — except at a distance, I mean — but there was a photo of him at Strathbeg, and it could be the same person. Poor Gilbert."

"It was a long war," he said, and then, with a hesitation that was unusual in him, "I didn't like to say anything before, but, well, you getting married and then losing him like that. I'm sorry."

"Thank you. It — well, it seems a bit like another life now. I was lucky to have what I did. And you, Davey? I'm surprised you're not married."

"Never got round to it. Never seemed to have the time."

"What sort of war did you have?"

"Oh, joined up as soon as I was eighteen — the DLI, of course, you were allowed your choice then if you were a volunteer. You'd just gone to college in Durham. There were four of us from the village, Arthur Barton and Pete Brigstock and Sid Telfer and me. You knew about Sid?"

"Yes."

"The four of us stayed together right through training, then we were drafted, and our battalion — the 16th, it was — was in Algiers by 1943. That's where Sid got his, at Sedjenane."

"I remember the news from there. It was rough, wasn't it?"

"Well, it wasn't a picnic. Pete got through it all without a scratch, and ended up in Italy, having a great time, according to him, en route to Greece." He laughed. "You should hear some of the things he has to tell, or come to think of it, maybe you shouldn't! To hear him now, it makes me sorry I missed out on the Greek bit."

"So don't miss out on what did happen. I know about Arthur. Do you mean you were wounded, too?"

"Nothing much." He was dismissive. "I

was back on active service in a matter of weeks, in time for D-Day. After that it was Normandy till the end of the war. Demobbed early this year. End of story."

"Yes. End of story." I was silent for a minute, remembering how lightly, almost, Davey and I had spoken of change. If the almost domestic traumas of my war had made something so different of me, what, then, of Davey? Back to Todhall and home and the old life? End of story?

I said, "Do you remember the shows Mr Lockwood used to put on in the village hall when we were little?"

"The magic lantern? Yes. They were great — at least we thought so then. Why?"

"I was remembering that slide he had, the kaleidoscope, where you turned a handle and all the bits of coloured glass got shaken up, and then fell into another pattern, a different one each time. Like the war. Shaking all our lives up into a different pattern, so different that we don't quite know what the pattern means."

He gave me a quick look I couldn't interpret, then he smiled. "We got shook up, no mistake about that, but I wouldn't worry too much about what the pattern is. Maybe it has changed a bit, but if you think about it, it's the same bits of glass every time."

"And that's a comfort?"

"It's meant to be, but take it or leave it."

Feeling, for some reason, vaguely lightened, I looked around me again at the big, calm beautiful room. "At any rate, this is still here, even if this sort of thing" — I lifted a hand — "is changing, too, Has changed already, everywhere."

"This sort of life, you mean? That's true. But this room isn't to be touched, just done up again. No change. Her ladyship's made sure of that."

"I'm glad. It's lovely, even though it's so grand — and so neglected. Do you know, I've never seen it before. I was never allowed in, even to dust."

"I'm not supposed to be in here now," he said cheerfully. "Come on. It's not worth going up into the south wing, it's still just a mess, and you can't really see what it'll be like. We haven't got much of a start yet. I'll just go up and get Dad's tool-bag, and I'll see you in the courtyard, and get you back for your date with the vicar."

We went back through the green baize door together.

17

As I went out into the sunshine of the courtyard, I heard the clatter of hoofs and the sound of a girl's laugh.

A few moments later two riders came in under the clock-tower arch, a man and a young woman. Neither of them, busy with their talk, noticed me, but I recognised the old flame of my childhood. Handsome Harry was still handsome, and his riding clothes, whipcord breeches and a yellow shirt with a silk cravat, suited him well. The girl was a good-looking blonde, beautifully turned out, who sat her horse well. A match for her escort, I thought, in more ways than one; she had a sort of smooth polish to movement and manner that could easily deal with men more worldly than Handsome Harry.

Before he could get round to help her dismount, she had thrown her right leg forward over the pommel and slid competently to the ground. He bent to loosen the girth, with some remark in an undertone, but she replied briefly and turned away, to see me sitting on the step of the mounting-block.

To my surprise, after a moment's fixed staring, her face lit up. "Kathy? Kathy Welland? It is Kathy, isn't it?"

I got to my feet. "Yes. But I'm afraid —?"

Laughing, she pulled off the peaked riding-cap and ran a hand through the fair hair. Harry had turned when she spoke, but she took no notice of him other than to throw him the reins of her horse. "Well? Now do you know me?"

"Prissy? It *is* Prissy? Oh my goodness me, where did you spring from?"

We flew together and kissed. The embrace was warmer than any we had exchanged in girlhood, but five years is five years, and there was a lot of time to make up. We clung to one another and laughed and asked questions and both talked at once while Harry, with the reins of both horses looped over one arm, hovered nearby, tapping his crop impatiently against a boot.

"Kathy Welland? Hullo, there!?"

"Hi, Harry." I threw it over my shoulder with a smile. "Nice to see you! Davey told me you were running the place here. It looks great. But Prissy, what on earth are *you* doing here in Todhall?"

"Just visiting, honey, just visiting! We're staying near Bishop Auckland with friends of Gordon's, and I don't play golf, so when someone said that Harry had started the stable up here, I came over on spec. But you, I might ask the same of you! What in the world brings you back here? I thought you'd shaken the dust off your feet years ago!"

I started to tell her, but at that moment Davey, with a tool-bag slung over one shoulder, came into the yard and made for his van. He gave Harry a nod, then glanced across at me, hesitating.

"He's giving me a lift back," I said to Prissy. "It's Davey Pascoe, you remember Davey?"

"Of course I do. I was here on Tuesday and I saw him and Mr Pascoe then. Hullo, Davey, how's it going?"

"Slowly. The hotel's supposed to open for Christmas, and dear knows if it will, but that's not our problem, and our bit of

the job should get done all right. Nice to
see you again, Pris. D'you want a lift now,
Kathy, or do you want to wait and get Pris
to take you back?"

"Oh, God, I can't," she said. "Kathy, I'm
sorry, but I'm due to join them at the Golf
Club and we're going on to drinks with
some people the Heslops know, and I've
got to get back to change. Look, I've just
got to see you, masses to talk about.
You're a rotten letter-writer and so am I.
How long are you here for and where are
you staying?"

"I'm at Rose Cottage, but I'll only be
there a day or two, just over the weekend."

"I could come there. I suppose you're
not even on the phone? No? Well, then,
we'll have to fix it now. What about tomorrow?"

"I thought you were coming riding
again," put in Harry.

"Well, I'm sorry, but I can't. It'll just be
the two days I owe you for. But thanks for
today, it was great."

"Why don't you both come?" he persisted. "The day after tomorrow? Satur-

day? We could go out by Low Beck, and get a good canter —"

"I can't ride," I said.

The familiar, charming smile. He really was very attractive. "I could teach you. I'd give you Maudie, she's very quiet, and we can forget the canter. You'd enjoy it." Then under his breath, but quite audibly, "And so would I."

"I'm sure I would. But I can't, thanks all the same." I turned back to Prissy, raising my voice above the sudden clatter as Davey threw the bag of tools into the back of the van, and slammed the doors shut. "And it's no good for us, either, I'm afraid, Pris. I'm packing the place up for Gran. She's at Strathbeg now, did you know? and she's decided to stay there. I've really only come to Todhall to get her stuff moved for her. Uncle Jim's fixing it with the movers for me, and he said something about Saturday, but I don't know yet. I'll be packing up tomorrow. So how about Monday? If the movers do come, we'll be a bit short of furniture, but we'll have a table and chairs and something to cook on, and what more do we want?"

"Sorry," she said, "I can't. We're leaving on Saturday. Tell you what, I'll come over tomorrow and give you a hand, and we'll go and eat somewhere good —"

"Such as?" I said, and laughed. "Spam sandwich at the Bull? You've forgotten, haven't you? Come over at lunch-time, anyway, and we'll eat at home, if I can remember to keep back some knives and forks. It'd be lovely to see you, and don't worry about the packing. Davey's going to help with that."

"Sure. Whatever you say. I'll be there."

Harry started to say something then, but just behind us Davey started up the van's engine, which was a noisy one.

"I've got to go," I said. "Nice to see you, Harry, and I hope things go well. You've a lovely place here. Tomorrow, then, Pris, any time you like, and that'll be wonderful. Okay, Davey, sorry to keep you waiting."

I climbed into the van, and we were off.

"Did you know Prissy Lockwood had friends at Bishop Auckland?" I asked him.

"Yes. Her husband and Major Heslop served together in the war. In Burma, I think. They go over there quite a bit, but this week's the first time I know of that she's been back to Toad Hall." A sidelong look that took me straight back to primary school. "Quite an Old Toddlers' Reunion, wasn't it? Do you think she came over here for Harry? She was always a bit sweet on him."

"Be your age, Davey, that was centuries ago, and anyway, it was just kids' stuff."

"For you, too?"

"For heaven's sake, I was in my teens, and as silly as they always are!" I rounded on him. "If it comes to that, what about you and Peggy Turner? You used to trail about after her like a puppy dog, and what you ever saw in her —!"

"Okay, okay, skinch!" *Skinch* was the local children's word for "pax", and I hadn't heard it for at least ten years. I laughed and, quite suddenly and for no reason that I knew of, felt like crying. I turned quickly to look out of the van window. The park stretched away, summer pasture studded with big trees, their lower branches, grazed flat by the cattle, stretching smoothly parallel to the ground. Each tree made its own island of shade, where sheep and cattle clustered.

No change here, not yet. The same yesterday, and today. But tomorrow?

Davey said no more as we turned out through the main park gates and rattled along the half mile that led to Lane Ends, the northern limit of the village street. No one was about. The place drowsed in the sun. The geese had disappeared, and Muffin was back by the pond. Cause and effect, no doubt.

"What time are you seeing the vicar?" asked Davey.

"Half past three, at the church."

"It's getting on for three now. If you like, you can wait at our place."

"No, no, I'll be fine. If you just put me down at the shop, I'll see what I can get for Prissy's lunch tomorrow, and then I'll sit in the sun till he comes."

"Okay. This do?"

"Yes thank you. Thanks again, Davey, I enjoyed it."

"Don't mention it. Do you still want me to come down and help with the packing-up tomorrow?"

"Yes, of course, if you have time."

"I'll have time. And if you come by the

workshop after you've seen the vicar, I'll run you home."

"Well, thank you, but —"

"See you," he said, and drove off.

I stared after him for a moment or two, then said something polite to Muffin, and went into the shop to see what I could find to feed Prissy on the morrow.

18

It was almost a quarter to four when the vicar at last came hurrying across the green into the churchyard, where I was sitting on the warm stone of the wall, waiting for him.

"I really am very sorry, Mrs Herrick, but we were over at Sedgefield for lunch, and then my wife needed the car, so I came home by bus, and the bus was late, and then there was someone waiting for me at the vicarage, and I simply couldn't get away. Have you been here long?"

"Not really, and anyway, who minds waiting on a day like this? I've enjoyed sitting in the sun."

"It is a lovely day, isn't it?" But he had hardly the air of anyone noticing. He wore his cassock, and carried a clean surplice over his arm. "Shall we go inside? The papers are in the vestry."

I slid from my perch and went with him. Inside the vestry it was cool and dim. He laid the clean surplice carefully over a chair, then took a key from a pocket and unlocked the old-fashioned safe — little more than a metal cupboard with a padlock — that stood in one corner. I caught a glimpse of books, registers, I supposed, stacked inside, and some objects wrapped in green baize that were presumably the Communion silver, and a cash box. He turned with a long manila envelope in his hand.

"Copies of what records we have," he said. "There may be others, but I looked up the dates you gave me, and came up with these."

"That's wonderful." I took the envelope. "Thank you very much."

"I was glad to be able to help. I did speak to Bob Crawley, by the way, and he told me some tale he had heard from the Miss Popes about a stranger at Rose Cottage this last weekend, but apparently he went all round the place and saw no sign of a break-in."

"I knew about that. Miss Mildred told me she thought she saw something, but that was all. I don't think it was anything to worry about."

"I'm glad to hear it." An inquiring look over the half-moon glasses. "Have you any clue yet as to what happened to the missing objects?"

"None at all. I've been asking around, but no one knows anything, and I'm sure the thief wouldn't be anyone local. Even if someone broke in and pinched the coins and medals and so on, they'd hardly take the papers, once they saw that the envelopes didn't hold cash. Well, thank you again, vicar. Is there — I mean, I think there's something called a search fee?"

"Indeed, indeed. I must charge you an exorbitant fee for my very valuable time." He smiled. "Six and eightpence, if you can manage it, and would be good enough to put it in the poor-box at the south door?"

"Of course. But if I may — there was just one more thing while I'm here —"

"Yes?" He had already turned away to pick up the surplice. Through the half-open door leading to the chancel I could hear sounds of people coming into the church. The christening party, presumably. I said quickly: "My grandfather's gravestone. My great-aunt is buried there, but they haven't yet put an inscription up. I wondered — they seem to have taken a very long time. I did wonder if my grandmother had forgotten to make arrangements for it, or if there had been a hold-up of some sort? I understand that the — well, the wording has to be approved by you?"

He stopped, with his head protruding from the neck of the surplice. With his hands sticking out of the sleeves he looked like a travesty of someone in the stocks. His spectacles had slipped right to the tip of his nose. Above them his eyes, unfocused, looked puzzled and, uncharacteristically, vague.

"I have no recollection of any letter from Mrs Welland, but I may be wrong. It is certainly some time since Miss Campbell died, and I would have thought . . . Oh dear. How remiss of me not to have followed it up sooner." A wriggle, and the surplice drifted into place. He pushed the straying spectacles back into place and straightened, in all the dignity of his robes.

"I think I hear the christening party now, so I must leave it, but if you like to go over to the vicarage and ask Lil to give you Paterson's address — it is beside the telephone in the hall — you can find out what if anything, has been arranged. In fact, I seem to recall Lil saying there had been an inquiry quite recently, so you may find that your grandmother has been in touch with Paterson herself. Or Mr Pascoe might know. Paterson is the stone-mason, and I am afraid he tends to be . . . shall we say dilatory? Please use my telephone if you wish — I know you have none at Rose Cottage."

I started to protest that there was no hurry, and that Mr Pascoe had already asked me about it, but he had turned away to gather his things together, with his eye on the vestry door, and his mind already on the party waiting at the font, where the star of the show could be heard already yelling blue murder. "Oh dear," he said, "one of those. Now if you will excuse me, Mrs Herrick —?"

"Of course. Thank you again. You're very kind. I won't forget the poor-box. Good afternoon, vicar."

I left by the outer door, amused to find myself automatically turning right off the gravel walk, following the rough grassy track that wound through the ancient gravestones to encircle the church. Another flicker of memory, rolling the years back. Coming out of Sunday School, ready for the long walk home — in those days one had run almost all the way — we children had always turned that way. One walked round a church clockwise, never widdershins. Just as one never stepped on the joins of paving-stones. And never forgot to cross one's fingers while telling a lie. And cried "skinch" to stop being teased or bullied . . .

Old Toddlers' Day.

The poor-box was in the south porch. I folded a ten-shilling note and pushed it through the slot. The child who had run all the way home to Rose Cottage had never seen a ten-shilling note in her life. So? That was then. This was now. I brought myself sharply back to the present and walked across to the vicarage.

I had not thought it worth telling the vicar that the stone-mason's number was on the letter-head of the paper Mr Pascoe had given me, but I wanted to see Lil, and preferably while there was no chance of coming across Mrs Winton Smith.

Lil was in the back yard, feeding the hens. She greeted me cheerfully, and I told her what the vicar had sent me for.

"Paterson's?" she said, looking surprised. "Your Auntie's grave? Well, yes, the number's there. Will I get it for you?"

"Don't bother, Lil, thanks. There's no hurry after all this time, but there was something else the vicar said, and I wanted to ask you about it."

She stood there in the sunshine with the bowl still half full of the hens' corn clutched to her breast. "Ask me?"

"Yes. He told me that there'd been someone else inquiring about the gravestone, fairly recently, he said. Do you remember?"

"Yes, I do. I was just thinking that it was funny, with her being buried all that time ago — I mind that, because she died just before I come here to work, and that was straight after I left school — and now you've come asked about it, when only last Sunday there was a man here asking the same thing."

Absurdly, in spite of the heat of the sun, I felt a shiver go over my skin. "Last Sunday? Do you know who he was? What did

he want to know? I gather he didn't speak
to the vicar?"

"No. He just come to the back door
here. He didn't want to see the vicar nor
the mistress, he just talked to me. I don't
know who he was, but he was a foreigner."

"A foreigner? Do you mean a real foreigner, or just a stranger to Todhall?"

"A real foreigner. He spoke funny. He
was a tall chap, thin, with a short kind of
coat, and —"

"He didn't give you his name, or say
where he was from?"

"No, miss."

"Could he — did he look like a gipsy?"

"Oh, no, miss. Well, I mean, he was
kind of sunburned, but his hair was grey,
and cut short, and his clothes . . . well,
they were foreign, too, but they looked
good, and he was a gentleman, for all he
spoke funny." She added, as if to prove
the point, "He come in a car."

"What did he say?"

"He asked what the vicar's name was,
and I told him, and did he want to see
him, because he was over at evening service and wouldn't be back till late, and so

was the mistress, but he said no. Then he asked who lived next door, and I said the Pascoes, but they were away for the weekend to a wedding. I said did he know them, and he said no again. Then he said about the grave, why wasn't there anything carved on it, and I said I didn't think anything had been arranged because there was nobody left to see about it since the old lady died and her sister had left and gone back home to Scotland. That was all, miss. Are you all right, miss?"

"Yes, thank you, I'm fine. Was there anything else?"

"I don't think so. I asked if I would tell the vicar and he said it didn't matter."

"And he never said where he was from, or what his interest was in the grave? Did he say . . . Did he mention Rose Cottage, for instance?"

"No, miss."

"And was he alone?"

"Well, I didn't see no one else, but I think there was someone in the car. He had a car outside the gate, and I thought I heard him talking to someone before it started up and drove away."

I was silent for so long that she began to look worried as well as curious, but then the cockerel created a diversion by flying up to grab food from the bowl she was carrying, and in the ensuing scuffle I took a pull at myself and managed to say, easily enough, "Well, thanks very much, Lil. It's certainly a bit odd and I'd love to know who the gentleman was, but he'll probably be in touch again, and if he knows I'm at Rose Cottage he can come to see me there. No, I won't come in. It doesn't matter about Paterson's, I'm sure their number's on the letter Mr Pascoe gave me. I'll not keep you, and thanks again. Goodbye."

And, parrying the offer of a cup of tea, I managed to get away and head for the workshop next door.

It was a long room, which had been a hay-loft in the days when the vicarage had owned and run its own farm. It was lighted mainly from windows let into the roof, but at one end there was a double door, used formerly for loading and un-loading, and this was open, letting in air and light. The floor was carpeted with shavings and sawdust, and the place smelled deliciously of pine and cedar and other woods, with undertones of varnish and linseed oil.

Davey was there, busy with a plane over a long piece of timber gripped by the vices on the bench that ran down the centre of the loft.

He glanced up when my shadow crossed the light, but without checking the smooth run of the plane along the plank's length. The sliver of wood, paper-thin and silvery, curled up and back, then floated down to join the sweet-smelling carpet on the floor. Davey straightened and turned.

"Well, did you get what you wanted from the vicar?"

"Yes. And something rather interesting from Lil at the vicarage."

"Oh?" He laid the plane down. "What was that?"

I told him about Lil's visitor, and he listened, head bent, while he ran a finger absently along the smooth surface of the planed wood. When I finished he gave a grunt and was silent for a few moments, then he said:

"And someone else in the car, eh? The lady?"

"Of course. And I am thinking what you're thinking."

"Such as?"

"Only that they went down to Rose Cottage and found it empty, and so they broke and entered. This man saw Lil during Sunday evensong, she says. So later, when Miss Linsey paid her visit to the cemetery, they were there."

"Again."

"Again?"

"Aye. They surely must have been at the grave earlier, before they came here to ask about the gravestone. Then they went back."

"Taking flowers for Aunt Betsy?"

"There's that, isn't there?" He turned and put the plane up the tool-rack that ran along one wall. "When your Mum was killed, was that gipsy with her?"

"I believe so. All I ever heard about it was what Aunt Betsy told me. I do know she said he was going to marry her, but Gran never knew his name, except she called him Jamie. There's nothing about the crash among the cuttings in her album."

"We could find out if we had to, I reckon. What I was thinking was, if he survived her, of if they'd parted before she died, then it's likely he'd marry again. Do gipsies 'talk funny'?"

"I've no idea. But if this was Jamie, and he'd come back for whatever reason to Todhall — to show it to the new wife or to look in the safe that my mother had told him about, or whatever — why, again why, the flowers for Aunt Betsy? And why take the papers from the safe? Why not just rob it?"

"From the sound of it, he'd not need to go stealing a few poundsworth from your Gran," said Davey. He reached his jacket down from its peg by the door. "We'll get no further by chewing things over now. Seems to me that what you need's a bit of time to see what the vicar's turned up for you, and then maybe start thinking about your Gran's packing."

"I suppose so."

"Whoever this chap is, if he's really bothered about anything in Todhall, he'll be back, and it would clear a whole lot of things up if you were there to talk to him . . . Prissy's coming to see you tomorrow, isn't she? Well, I'll be along in the afternoon to give you a hand, so don't try shifting anything, just get the small stuff sorted ready. Coming?"

I came.

19

He took me back through the park, and set me down by the bridge, refused the offer of tea — "I'll get mine at half-six when I've done" — and then drove off.

As soon as I was in the house with the door shut I saw down at the table and pulled the vicar's envelope out of my pocket.

It was a meagre crop, though I supposed it was worth six and eightpence of the vicar's time. The first was the copy of my grandparents' marriage certificate: Henry Welland, gardener, to Mary Campbell, domestic servant, witnessed by Jeremiah Pascoe, carpenter, and Giles Brandon, farmer — "farmer" being the accepted label for the owners of the land, the gentry. I had heard it all from Gran, of course, how Sir Giles had not only attended the ceremony, but had made a speech at the wedding breakfast in the village hall, and given the young couple the tenancy of Rose Cottage, which had "just been done up lovely" after the death of its previous occupant.

Then, a decent year and a half later, the certificate of baptism of Lilias Mary, their daughter, with the godparents duly noted, Margaret and Jeremiah Pascoe.

Why I should have hoped for anything from the next slip of paper I do not know. It was some years now since I had rummed up my courage and written to Somerset House, and I had my own copy of my birth certificate, but I sat there staring at the vicar's careful copperplate as if something might be written there between the lines. It was the certificate of baptism of Katherine Mary, daughter of Lilias Welland. Father unknown. And the godparents, friends to the third generation, James and Annie Pascoe, with Sybilla Lockwood, the vicar's wife.

And that was all. I bestirred myself at length. I got up and went to lift the Unseen Guest down from the wall and push the papers into the safe.

I had barely readjusted the framed text when there was a knock at the door.

I suppose I stood there for a full ten

seconds, my hands still on the frame, tightening till the knuckles showed white. My first thought was, *It's the foreigner, the gipsy, he's here already, the stranger who's been asking questions about my family — now perhaps I'll find out some of the things I want to know.* My second, *I wonder if I want to hear them after all?* And finally, as I pried my hands loose from the Unseen Guest and turned to the door, *And Davey's back at home by now, and a good two miles away . . .*

I opened the door.

It was no foreigner, though the woman who stood there was something of a stranger. I had not seen her for some time, but she never seemed to change. The elder Miss Pope, Agatha. And behind her was Miss Mildred.

"Well, how nice to see you, Miss Agatha!" I said, and relief must have warmed my voice into such a delighted welcome that she looked surprised. "And Miss Mildred, too. How good of you to call! Do please come in."

"I know it's not Friday," said Miss Mildred, following her sister into the room.

"She means," said Miss Agatha, "that

normally she only walks to meet my train on Friday. But we've been in Sunderland to the pictures, and Sister persuaded me to come here with her on our way home because she was worried, and wanted to talk to you."

"Oh?" I said, at a loss. "Well, please sit down, won't you? I'm sorry the place is a bit untidy, but I've been trying to sort things out for the movers. Would you like a cup of tea? It won't take a minute, I was just going to put the kettle on anyway."

"No, thank you. We always have high tea when we've been into town, and it is all laid ready." She sat down, still holding her handbag firmly on her lap, as if ready to go at any moment. I took my place by the table again, and she fixed me, much as the Ancient Mariner fixed the Wedding Guest, with her glittering spectacles. Miss Mildred, perched on the edge of the rocking-chair, made a little chirping sound like a nervous young bird. I began to feel a little nervous myself. Perhaps the strange foreigner would have been a little less alarming.

Miss Agatha spoke in her deep, rather pleasant voice.

"My sister wanted me to come with her to tell you," she said, "though I have no idea what she is talking about. It's very difficult, but I always say that when a thing is difficult or unpleasant one had better say it at once."

I'll bet you do, I thought, and said aloud: "Oh, dear. Well, you're probably right. So what is it, please?"

"Only that Miss Linsey is insisting now that she saw your mother here in Todhall last Sunday night. In the graveyard," said Miss Agatha, and shut her lips tight on the word.

A twitter from Miss Mildred, then I said, "But I know that. She told me herself."

"My sister was afraid —" began Miss Agatha, but Miss Mildred rushed in, the blue eyes filling with tears, the kindly face flushed.

"Poor Bella. Her dreams, it's those wretched — I mean those dreams of hers she thinks are visions. She lets them upset her so . . . Well, you remember I told you that I thought there had been someone here, at Rose Cottage, with a light, on Monday night?"

"Yes, of course I remember."

"Well, I wasn't thinking, and I told Bella what Bob Crawley had said, about someone digging there near the toolshed, and I said, 'Perhaps it was your ghosts, Bella,' quite without thinking, and she looked so queer, and said, you know the way she does, 'A warning. It could be a warning. Sometimes even the unenlightened are used to warn of a death,' and she just put her cup down and went without another word. She was having tea with me at the time."

"When was she not?" said Miss Agatha, under her breath.

Miss Mildred swept on without pausing. I thought I could acquit her of wanting to pass on disturbing news, but if it had to be done, then she would get it over as quickly as possible. "I'm afraid I put it out of my mind, because, well, you know Bella, but it kept coming back to worry me, so I told Sister, and she said it was far better to tell you ourselves than for Bella perhaps to come down here frightening you with her tales."

"As a matter of fact —" I began.

"Go on. If you're going to tell her, tell her," said Miss Agatha firmly, with a brave disregard for both her sister's feelings and mine.

Miss Mildred gulped, then said distress-fully, "It's just that I had this feeling" — she waved a hand somewhere near what I was sure she would have called her bosom — "that it was all my fault that Bella got the idea that someone was here digging a grave, as if it wasn't bad enough for you to have to listen to all the other" — a pause — "the other *stuff* about your poor mother in the cemetery."

For Miss Mildred, the word was an ex-pletive. And with it she had apparently shot her bolt. She sat back, dabbing at her eyes. I gave her a smile which she didn't see, but Miss Agatha looked sud-denly interested.

"You knew this already." She made it a statement, not a question.

"Yes. Thank you for coming to tell me, it was kind of you, but actually Miss Lin-sey did come here last night, and we had a talk. We — well, we got her dream sorted out, I think."

"Well, really!" Miss Agatha's deep voice went deeper. She added, rather unfairly, "If that isn't just like her! Anything to get something frightening off her chest and onto yours! I never did hold with all that nonsense of Bella's. She'll be breathing ectoplasm next."

"I don't think one actually — that is, never mind, but look, Miss Agatha," I said hurriedly, "whatever Miss Linsey thought it might mean, or whatever Bob Crawley said about the digging, there's nothing to it, really. I went and took a look myself yesterday. It's true that someone has been digging there recently, over by the tool-shed, but —"

Another tiny sound from Miss Mildred, and a deep, "Really?" from her sister.

"Yes, but it's not a grave, nothing like one, it's just a small patch that's been dug over. Nothing there. I told Miss Linsey that, and she seemed quite ready to dismiss it. Dismiss it, I mean, as not being anything to do with her vision, or dream, or whatever you like to call it . . ." I turned a hand over. "But not, I'm beginning to think, not nonsense, Miss Agatha."

"Indeed? Well?"

I leaned forward in my chair. "Look, let's get one thing clear. It's obvious that whatever these dreams of Miss Linsey's may mean, it's nothing to do with my mother or with me here and now. She died years ago. And it's even longer since she was here in Todhall. Even if she were still alive, and came back here, would anyone recognise her straight away like that, and in the dark, too?" I drew a breath. "Listen. There's something I think I ought to tell you, but for the present, please may we keep it between ourselves till I find out more about it? I heard today that a man called here recently, at the vicarage, asking about the grandfather's gravestone, and he had a friend with him."

"Ah!" That was from Miss Agatha. "A woman?"

"I don't know. It could be. If so, it's possible that it was that couple Miss Linsey saw in the cemetery."

"Do you know who he was?"

"No. A stranger to Todhall, apparently. It was Lil who answered the door to him."

"And she's not been here very long herself. A stranger to the village? So what was his interest, do you suppose, in your grandfather's grave?"

"It's Aunt Betsy's, too." In face of that intelligent, unwinking stare I did not feel like taking the thing any further, and said merely, "Davey Pascoe and I went up there today with flowers, and there were some already on Aunt Betsy's grave. They could have been put there on Sunday."

"Connections of Betsy Campbell's. I see. Yes." A final, summing look at me that apparently decided her to leave the subject. "Ah, well." And Miss Agatha, stiff, deep-voiced, still braced with disapproval of the whole world of dreams and visions and ghosts from the past, sounded re-signed, rather than relieved. "Well, Mil-dred, it seems as if Bella may have been right, even if misguided."

"Poor Bella. She has been so dis-tressed." That, tremulously, from Miss Mildred, and it brought a snort from her sister.

"Then she might at least have kept it to herself! It's a mercy that Kathy here has so much sense."

"Don't worry about me," I said. "But I must say I hope Miss Linsey isn't going around telling her story to everyone in the village!"

"I doubt if she will. She is in some ways," finished Miss Agatha, with (I thought) considerable restraint, "a difficult neighbour. But I think I can assure you, Kathy, or should I call you Mrs Herrick now?"

"Kathy is fine."

"I can assure you that this won't go any further. We only came to tell you about it because Millie here has been so upset, and we did not know what Bella had already said to you. And you need not worry that she will go about repeating her nonsense in the village — for nonsense it is, whether true or not," she finished robustly. "I have spoken to her myself."

And I'll bet that puts paid to any more dreams for a fair while, I thought, then was afraid I had said it aloud, because Miss Agatha smiled suddenly, her eyes twinkling behind her spectacles. "I'll see that it does," she said. "And I'm sure you are far too sensible to lose any sleep over it. Come, Millie."

They went.

Sensible or not, I did lose a fair amount of sleep that night, but morning came safely at last, and brought Prissy, elegant, laughing, and laden with goodies for lunch.

20

She had brought smoked salmon and some fresh rolls, and a bag of peaches.

"I didn't think Barlow's shop would be stocking these quite yet," she said cheerfully, dumping them on the kitchen table. "And I won't tell you where I got them. The blackest of markets, needless to say, but it's my conscience, not yours, and I've had more practice with that than you, being a vicarage child. I keep my conscience in my stomach these days, anyway. Here, I brought a lemon, just in case. There's a tin of ham, too, but since you'd asked me to lunch I thought I could leave the main course to you. You used to be a good cook before you went up in the world."

"Stewed rabbit," I said, and then laughed at her carefully expressionless face. "No, don't worry. There's no one to shoot the poor little beggars now. It's chicken."

"Well, thank goodness for that! I thought

that heavenly smell couldn't be rabbit! So there's a black market here in deepest Todhall, too?"

"Only pale grey. I was lucky. I remembered Mr Blaney used to do a poultry round on Fridays, and I got a spare. Oh boy, this salmon looks wonderful! Thank you! That makes it a feast. Drink first? I scrounged some reasonable sherry from the Black Bull. Now, canny lass, sit thisel' doon, and for a start, tell me how you got that gorgeous figure, Podgy Pris?"

"Doing without smoked salmon and roast chicken. Years, just *years,* my dear, of disgusting things like raw cabbage and carrots and home-made yoghourt. But it's worth it in the end. It's Slim Scilla now. Thanks. Cheers." She raised her glass and sipped sherry. "Not bad, for Todhall! Yes, Gordon won't have me called Prissy any more, I'd have you know." She laughed. "I went up in the world too, my girl! I didn't see it like that at the time, because I fell for Gordon in a big way before I knew anything about him, but marrying a wealthy banker is definitely a step up from any vicarage you care to name!"

I laughed. "I believe you! Scilla? It's

pretty. Same with me. I'm Kate to all Jon's friends, but somehow now I'm back here Kathy comes more natural. And so, I'm afraid, does Prissy."

"Fair enough. So long as you forget the Podgy bit!"

"How could I even think it, seeing you now? Hang on a minute while I look at the chicken . . . Yes, it's about ready. Now, we've a lot to catch up on. Tell me all about it. I know you got some sort of teaching job after Gordon was sent overseas, and then the school was evacuated to Canada. When was he demobbed, and are you settled over here now, and where are you living? Heavens, we have lost touch, haven't we? Your mother and I keep up, of course, Christmas and birthdays and such, but I don't really know a thing about you, except that you're happy, and now that you and Gordon are together she's dying to enter the Granny stakes. Any hope for her?"

"Not up and running yet, but her name's down." She laughed, stroking a hand down over her flat stomach. "Podgy Pris will soon be with us again."

"Well, that's wonderful. When?"

"Oh ages, Christmas, and you will be godmother, won't you? We mustn't lose touch again. You're surely not thinking of living here? I heard about Aunt Betsy, but I don't know — I mean, how's your grand-mother? Is she —"

"Still alive? Sure. She went back to Scotland after Aunt Betsy died. She's fine, at least she's in bed just now getting over the flu, but she'll be with us, please God, for a lot of years yet. Look, shall we start on the salmon?"

"I brought some brown rolls. They're in that bag. I hope you've got some butter, or is it still Gran's marg?"

I laughed as I set the dish on the table. We had always been able to say things like that without offending. "Here you are, ma'am. They make their own at Strathbeg, and Gran gave me some to bring. Help yourself, there's a whole half-pound."

It was a delightful meal. There was five full years' news and gossip to make up. She knew only the barest facts about my marriage, and, cut off as I had been from my childhood's friends, I had never talked about it before, that brief, frantic span of my life, when I had spun from rapture (I had loved him dearly) to dread, the nights that were not passed with him spent wakeful, listening for the planes overhead, trying, uselessly and without comfort, to count them, the number going out, the lesser number returning. And then the final grief, the long-expected, numbing blow that stops the pain and brings a kind of relief. Life had stopped. Life would have to go on. Life went on, and in time the unbelievable began to happen; pleasure and happiness came back, and even joy. But love? Not again. I said it very firmly. Not again.

"Not anyone?" she asked.

"It's just that I don't think that could happen to me again. It would be different now, love would, I mean. I'm older, and want different things. Coffee? It's Barlow's best, which isn't exactly fresh-ground, but it's quite okay."

After coffee we washed up, then wandered outside into the sunshine, down to the gate and on to the bridge. The sun was hot on our backs as we leaned elbows on the railing and gazed down into the clear, sliding depths below.

"There's one! Look over there, in the

shadow of that stone. Do you remember when we came looking for eels, and Davey Pascoe fell into the beck and broke your grandfather's rod, and got thrashed for it?"

The flood of memories, as deep and clear as the stream below us, took us well into the afternoon, till Prissy, looking at her watch, said reluctantly, "I'd better be going, I suppose, We're leaving tomorrow. Gordon has to be in London for two or three nights. How long did you say you'd be here? And will you go back to London, or up to your Gran's?"

"I'll go north first, to see her settled with all her stuff, and I'll stay, if she'll let me, till she's out and about again. Look, won't you stay a bit longer, and have some tea?"

"I really can't."

"Well, come back in and get your bag, and we can exchange addresses. Would you like some flowers?"

We had been making our way back as we spoke, and she had paused at the gate, where the roses and honeysuckle had gone wild along the fence.

"Love some. Hotel bedrooms are kind

of soulless, and I haven't been back in England long enough to get used to these heavenly gardens."

"Half a minute while I get the scissors."

When I got back into the garden she was over by the toolshed. "This rose! Isn't it just lovely? Would it last if I took some?"

"Not long, but it's worth it. I'll cut it in bud, and that should get it to London with you. Take care, it's pretty prickly, and I'm not sure if these scissors are strong enough. Ought to have secateurs, really, but they've gone. Gran gave the tools away to Davey."

"Well don't bother, then. It's a sweet rose, and they must have been pretty fond of it. They're all the same in this corner, even the one that's been dug up. There's the label, look, under those weeds." She picked it up and handed it to me.

I took it. A small metal label, embossed with a name, CHINA: OLD BLUSH. A label that had presumably fallen from the bush when it was dug up, and which had been flung aside among the weeds when I, in my turn, had dug in the same spot.

I stood there, staring down at the thing

in my hand. So that was it, the solution
of Miss Mildred's mystery, the light in the
cottage garden, the man digging. That la-
borious job, done with the clumsy coal
shovel, was not a grave, for buried treasure or anything else. He had simply been
digging up a rose-bush.

Why?

I knew the answer, of course, even if I
could give no reason for it. To take it to
the cemetery and replant it on the grave.

"And if he shifted it at this time of the
year, no wonder if looked as if it was dying for lack of water."

"What was?" asked Prissy curiously.
"What are you talking about?"

"I'm sorry. I was thinking aloud. It's
nothing, just a sort of mystery that keeps
cropping up, but probably doesn't mean a
thing."

"Well, if it doesn't, it seems to worry
you just the same. You looked for a minute there as if you were sleep-walking.
Want to tell me?"

So I told her, standing there by the toolshed, and turning the little label over and
over in my hand.

She only interrupted once, to say, "Huh!

Witches' Corner! Doesn't change, does it?" when I got to Miss Linsey and the sisters, but when I had finished she was vehement.

"Well, of all the silly old cuckoos! What do they think they were doing, coming down with you here on your own, to chew it all over again? Were you frightened? I'd be scared witless, anyway, sleeping down here by myself."

"No, I'm not scared, I like it here. Confused certainly, and maybe a bit nervous, but I don't honestly think there's anything to be scared about. All it comes to is that this man, presumably, must be the one who broke in and took the things from the wall-safe. Heaven knows who, or why. And if he really did dig up one of these roses and take a whole lot of flowers over for Aunt Betsy —" I dropped the label back on the weeds, and dusted my hands together. "Well, it's another piece in the puzzle, and no doubt they'll all fit in the end."

"I hope so, I must say!" said Prissy, "It's all a bit weird, but I think you're right, it sounds pretty harmless to me, and so do old Linsey-woolsey's fancies. So forget them. Anyway, you'll soon be away and out of it all." A shrewd look. "Am I right in detecting a bit of nostalgia, a bit of the Old Toddler, about you? Well, it's been fun, but forget it, chum. Get back to London, and central heating and telephones, and get on with your real life. There's nothing for you here."

"You may be right. But I'm here for a day or two anyway. And I'm sure there's nothing really to worry about. Mysteries don't go well with Todhall and Granddad's roses."

"If you're sure you're all right —"

"I'm sure. If I do get scared I can always go to the Pascoes. You've got my addresses — London and Strathbeg? Great. It's been lovely, Prissy, and don't let's lose touch again, especially with your interesting news coming up! Take care, and thanks again for everything. 'Bye."

21

Davey came down soon after Prissy had gone, with the information that the removers had telephoned to his mother to say they would come next day.

"Saturday?" I exclaimed. "I didn't think they could possibly come before Monday!"

"Seems they have an urgent delivery at Sedgefield, so Mr Caslaw told them to save a journey and do the pick-up here on the way home. Costs him no more, and they don't mind, getting time and a half. So they'll be here tomorrow morning, and we'd better get going."

He had brought a packet of coloured stick-on labels, and while I made tea he toured the kitchen and backplaces with Gran's list in his hand, affixing the labels to the things that were to be removed. It was left to me to finish sorting out the small objects that were not on the list, but which I thought she might want, so, after clearing away and washing up our tea-cups, I did a final rummage through drawers and cupboards, and then turned my attention to the contents of the cupboard under the stairs.

"Not much to go from upstairs," said Davey, scanning the list. "You'll still have somewhere to sleep. And not much from your Gran's room either. I suppose she took her best stuff up when she left?"

"I don't think so. No furniture, at any rate. She was sleeping at the Lodge to begin with. Anyway, the beds and things aren't worth taking. They've been here since the Flood. Aunt Betsy had the best of the bedroom furniture."

"She would."

I laughed. "To be fair, Gran did her room up before she came. There are one or two things there that came from the Hall, and they're good. They're on the list."

"Yeah." He was studying Gran's rather uncertain writing. "Here we are. 'B's room. Wee table with gate leg by the bed. Chest of drawers. Chair with green velvet. Glass vase. Pic of the Hall. Mat beside bed. Landing clock.' What on earth's a landing clock?"

"The clock on the landing, what else?"

"As you say, what else? Well, I'll go and mark them, shall I? Which was her room?"

"Second left at the top of the stairs. The clock's beside the door."

"Okay."

I finished with the stair-cupboard, then turned to emptying out what was left in the sideboard drawers, with a view to re-packing in them as many as possible of the small things that Gran had not thought to list, but which I knew she would like to have. The candlesticks from the mantel-piece, the rose vases, the china ducks; all these, carefully wrapped in newspapers and old tea-towels, went to join the tea-set, the "best" cloths, the half-dozen silver teaspoons that had been a wedding pres-ent from the Pascoes. I was tipping the contents of the bottom drawer out on the table when I became, gradually as it were, conscious of complete silence from up-stairs.

I stopped work and listened. No move-ment, nothing. I had just taken breath to call out when his voice came:

"Kathy."

"Yes?"

"Come here a minute."

"What is it?"

"Just come up here."

I went with some reluctance. I had not been into the big front bedroom since I had been back at Rose Cottage. But I need not have worried that anything of Aunt Betsy's presence would be left there. The room was stripped and clean, and smelling of the polish Mrs Pascoe had used. The bed was bare, covered only by the mattress, the only soft furnishings being the cotton curtains and the "mat beside bed", which was, in fact, a worn but still lovely Oriental rug, that had been a gift from Lady Brandon. This was lying, folded as small as it would go, on the bare mattress, and beside it was one of the drawers from the chest. This was empty. Davey was sitting on the bed, with a paper in his hand. Not the list; this had floated to the floor by his feet. It was a ragged slip of paper, yellow with age.

"Davey? What on earth is it? You look queer."

He got to his feet, lifting the empty drawer, and sliding back into its place. "I feel queer. Sit down. I've found something you'll want to see."

I sat down on the bed. I knew already what was in his hand. It could only be a newspaper cutting, the paper whose absence from the family chronicle was so remarkable. I put out a hand and he gave it to me, then turned and went over to the window, where he stood with his back to me, looking out.

It was indeed a cutting, from a West of Ireland newspaper. The date, 12 January 1931. The heading, *Two Die In Bus Crash,* then, told in the bare local-news style, the story of a country bus trundling home late on a dark night, empty of all but its last two passengers as it neared the end of its journey, and colliding with a bullock that was straying, black and invisible in that black night, across the unfenced road. The bus had swerved, skidded, then plunged down the steep roadside bank, where it had overturned, and burned. It was (said the report) no fault of the driver's; he was new to the route, and in spite of a broken arm and multiple bruises he had done his best to drag his passengers from the burning bus, but they were beyond help. Mr and Mrs Smith, said the *Sligo Advertiser,* had only recently arrived in Ireland, where Mr Smith was employed at the stables of the well-known Flaherty brothers. Mr P. Flaherty himself had identified the remains, and the relatives in England had been informed of the tragedy.

And that was it.

"Smith's a gipsy name, isn't it?" I said at length. "And no address for them except the stables. Maybe they'd settled down to live there, after they left the travelling people. Yes. It happened two years after she left home." I took a breath, with something like relief. "So they were still together, and he did marry her. That's something, isn't it? And it tells us something else, too. The 'foreign gentleman' at the vicarage wasn't my mother's gipsy after all. So we'll still have to wait to find who he was. Well, I'm glad to have this, Davey. Where did you find it?"

"At the back of the drawer. The chest's empty, so I thought I'd pack the small stuff into the drawers. The linen and stuff that she wanted from her own room, and —" he turned from the window towards me. I couldn't see his face properly, but his voice sounded flat and strained — "it was in an envelope, and stuck to the back of the drawer. Deliberately stuck, I mean. Meant to be hidden."

"Well, I'm glad you found it. I've wondered why there was nothing about the accident in Gran's album. Maybe she didn't want to be reminded. If that's the case I won't tell her about it, but I'll keep it anyway." I tried for a light tone. "Have you ever read *Northanger Abbey,* Davey?"

"No."

"The heroine in that thinks she's in the middle of a 'horrid mystery', and she finds a paper in a cabinet in her bedroom, but it's only a laundry list. At least this paper's part of our mystery, even if it doesn't tell us —"

"There's other papers."

His tone, as much as the words, struck the breath from me, and the words from my mouth. He took two strides across from window to bed and was standing over me.

"Here," he said, and laid a torn, dirty envelope in my lap, then went quickly from the room, and I heard him go downstairs two at a time. The front door opened and shut.

I sat there in the silence for what seemed like half an hour or so, but was probably only a minute. Was this, at last, the fact I had tried to search out? Something known to Aunt Betsy, but kept from Gran, and used to drive my mother, the despised sinner, out of the Christian home, and prevent her from corrupting her child? I found that my hands were shaking as I drew out the contents of the envelope.

They were letters, one of them still in its envelope, held together by a twist of what I recognised as Aunt Betsy's embroidery wool. It was rotten, and snapped easily, and I dealt the papers out onto the mattress in order, as one might deal Patience cards.

The first letter was in a flimsy envelope with an American stamp. The address on the back was, one could guess, a boarding-house. The letter was not dated, but the postmark was clear. July 1932.

More than a year after the bus crash.

* * *

So here at last were the first lines of the story that was later to come clear, a story of spite and bigotry, too mean and petty to be called tragedy, but tragic for all that.

He had married her, the gipsy boy, and they had had a couple of years together, living any way they could, until there had come the chance of the job in Ireland, and they had left the travelling folk and Jamie had landed the job at the Flaherty stables. Until that move, as I knew, she had tried to keep in touch, cards at Christmas and birthdays, then, after the date of the bus crash, silence.

The letters told why.

In the first of these she told of their journey to Ireland, along with another young couple from "Jamie's folk," their friends. The friends had not been so lucky with a job as Jamie, but Jamie stayed with the Flahertys for less than two months. A visiting American racehorse-owner had liked his way with horses, and had offered him a good job "back home", fare provided. Jamie, gipsy that he was, had not troubled to see out his notice. He and Lilias had faded into the night and taken the next ship across, telling no one of their plans except Jamie's friend, who was still looking for a job.

So much for the facts that could be gleaned from the letter. The rest could be guessed at. The couple in the burned-out bus must have been the other gipsy pair, perhaps hoping to pick up Jamie's job. Unknown in the district, unrecognisable anyway, the burned bodies were, probably naturally, assumed to be Jamie and Lilias, taking that last bus home.

There were four more letters. In the first of these she told of her marriage, not long after Jamie's death in 1934 from a virus pneumonia, to an American businessman — "very respectable from Ioa". It was his third marriage, and there were two children at home. From the brief sentence at the end — "Ive not told him nothing" — it could be gathered that the very respectable gentleman from Iowa did not yet know of his pretty wife's previous slip-up. Me.

The next letter was the shocking one.

"Dear Mum,
      I got your letter aunt B wrote for you and I wish I hadn't. I know you think

I am wicked and not fit to be near Kathy but it is hard to be told never to see you again. I wish you had writen me after Jamie died. He wasnt much but he was good to me and now Im married again to Larry a good man and he does not know what I did and you dont have to worry as I am living in America and rich. Please give Kathy a kiss from me and tell her to grow up a good girl and not like her mum and take care. I wish I could see you again but I know you are right that I mustnt show my face in Todhall ever again as Kathy has to grow up re-spectable.

Your loving Lil."

The next was very brief, just to ask why her mother had not replied, and the last was the same, a sad little missive with a ring of farewell about it. She understood, and just wanted her mother to know that she was happy, and got on well with her husband's family, and to forget her. She did understand, and it was for Kathy's sake, and please give Kathy a kiss . . .

I sat for a long time with the letters in

my lap, thinking about it, and how it could
have happened. Aunt Betsy, obviously,
had intercepted the letters. Keeping house
here at Rose Cottage, with Gran working
daily up at the Hall, she could easily have
done so. Even the postman could not
have guessed that the American letters,
labelled as they would be with Lilias's
married name, were from Gran's "dead"
daughter.

That first letter from America must (I
thought) have come like a bomb. The
sender's name on the back — Mrs L Smith
— would be enough to set Aunt Betsy
guessing, and must have led her to open
the letter, to find that against all reason
Lilias was still alive and well. What to do?
Pass on the glad news and then wait for
the prodigal's welcome home? Or keep
quiet for the moment, and wait?

To start with, she might only have been
concerned to keep Lilias the sinner away
from Gran and me, but it was also possible that she was afraid — with reason —
that if Lilias ever should come home, she
herself would be turned out. So she had
kept quiet, and waited.

Then the second letter came, and with

it, no doubt, relief. Jamie was dead, but Lilias was still in America — in those days a safe enough distance away — and had remarried and was settled there. Aunt Betsy must have thought that there was no longer any risk of her "coming back to life", and perhaps returning to Todhall to usurp her, Betsy's, place. She had made sure of it; she had written, as she sometimes did for Gran, to tell Lilias that she would never be welcome at home again; that Todhall wanted none of her; that as far as her home was concerned, she was dead. And through it all, Gran had been allowed to believe that her daughter had in fact died years ago.

I got up from the bed slowly, moving like an old woman, and went downstairs. Davey must have been watching for me. He came in, and without word or pause, walked right up to me and put his arms round me tightly, patting my shoulder. It was a brotherly sort of comfort, and I assured myself that it was exactly what I wanted.

"It's all right, love," he was saying, "it's all right."

"Davey, you read the letters."

"Yes."

"It's — I haven't taken it in yet. But did you see what's written on the back of the envelope?"

"No."

He let me go, and I showed it to him. Aunt Betsy's writing. *The Wages of Sin Is Death.*

"But it isn't," said Davey, robustly. His hands came out again to take me by the arms and shake me gently. "That's just what it isn't! It's all good news, couldn't be better, so never you mind what that wicked old woman got herself up to! What all this really means is that your Mum is still alive! I know you've been having thoughts about it, with all these queer happenings lately, and so have I! And now it's true. D'you get it? Alive! Alive and kicking and somewhere near Todhall! Come on, Kathy love, dry your eyes! You got a hanky?"

"Yes. Yes, I know. I know. That's twice you called me love," I said, into the hanky.

"What?"

"Nothing," I said, rubbing my eyes dry, and smiling at him.

"Listen, then! Work it out, now that we

know. She's been here, back to Todhall, with the American husband, the foreigner. They come here — this is Sunday night — find the cottage empty, and your Gran gone. So they make for the village, and on the way they stop at the cemetery to visit your granddad's grave, and there's another grave, and no name yet on the stone. What d'you bet she thinks it's her Mum, and then that girl at the vicarage puts the lid on it —"

"That's it!" I exclaimed. "If she said what she said to me — 'The old lady died and the sister went back home to Scotland' — then they might easily take it that it was Gran who'd died and Aunt Betsy who'd gone back north. I noticed myself the way she put it, because Jinnie at the shop, Lil's friend, used the same turn of phrase, and it sounded odd to me."

"She could easily take it that way. If my folks had been at home she might have come to our house, and saved us a deal of trouble." A short laugh. "But they weren't, and your Mum maybe didn't want to show her face in the village yet, so she stayed in the car and he did the asking, and got put on the wrong tack by Lil Ashby."

"Well," I said, "we got one thing right — she'd never have taken flowers for Aunt Betsy."

"I doubt if she'll ever get any now after this. But she did get a bit of what she deserved, if you think about it."

"What? You mean that my mother got married to a respectable gentleman in the end?"

"That he was rich," said Davey briefly. "She says so, doesn't she, in one of those letters?"

"So she does. My poor Mum, she can't be very happy right this minute, coming back here after all this time, and thinking her mother's died."

"All the better, when she finds the bad news isn't true after all," he said cheerfully. "So there's the story, all but the end. They came down here from the vicarage, and cleared the safe out — she'd know where your Gran kept the key — and then they got some flowers for what they thought was your Gran's grave —"

"And dug up one of Granddad's roses," I said, and told him about it.

"With the coal-shovel," he said, and laughed. "Her rich American gentleman. I'd have liked to have seen that! But hang on a minute. If they robbed the safe — it must have been them — they didn't do that till Monday. Why not?"

"Because 'Davey Pascoe has got your Granddad's tools.' I quote. I've been told that every ten minutes since I got home."

"And they couldn't cut the plaster without them. Right. So they went and got something to do the job with, and came back next evening. Yes. That's it." He paused, seemed about to say something else, then repeated, "Well, that's it."

I sat down by the table and stared at him over the litter of stuff from the sideboard drawer that I had tipped there. Shock, amazement, relief, anxiety and a cautious happiness — a rush of contrasting emotions had left me confused and exhausted.

"And now they've gone. How do we find them again? What do we do?"

"Wait," he said, cheerfully. "What else? Wait here. There's still you. You can't tell me she'll give up without trying to find you. And Todhall's the only starting-point she has. What's the betting that if you sit tight here she'll be back again?"

"Yes," I said. "Yes, of course. I — I can't grasp it, Davey. I — if she comes back here . . . And then there's Gran. We'd better not say anything to Gran yet, till we know for sure." I shook my head as if to shake my brain back into action. "Oh, heavens alive, if it is true, how on earth do I tell Gran?"

"If I was you," he said, "I'd stop thinking about it and get myself some supper. Have you got some food, or will I take you home again?"

"No. There's plenty. We had a chicken for lunch. Davey —" I hesitated.

"I know. You want a bit of time to yourself. That's okay. Just remember, this kind of news doesn't kill. Your Gran'll be out of her bed and skipping like a spring lamb, just like you'll be yourself once it's sunk in. But till we're sure, say nowt. Don't worry, I'll not tell Mum and Dad yet . . . Well, if you're sure you're all right, I'll get along. Okay?"

"Yes. But Davey —"

He turned in the doorway. "What?"

"Thanks for everything. I don't know what I'd do without you."

"You don't have to," he said. At least, that is what I thought he said, and I thought he added "Love", as he wheeled abruptly away and went down the path. The gate creaked shut. The van door slammed. The engine coughed into life and the van moved off.

I went to cut myself some of the cold chicken for supper.

22

The cottage felt very empty after Davey had gone. It seemed to give off an echo like that in a long-deserted house.

Well, I thought, as I finished my solitary supper and washed the dishes, what now? Prissy had been adamant in urging me to go back to London, to "life" as she called it, as soon as the furniture removers had been, but now, of course, I would have to stay. If Davey and I were right about the mystery, and my mother was really still alive and somewhere in the vicinity, she would surely come back to Rose Cottage again.

Part of me longed for her coming, with a kind of uncertain excitement, but another part was afraid. Afraid of time, of change, of what had happened to us both in the lost years. And, however joyfully the news of her daughter's reappearance must come to Gran, I did not know how to break it to an ailing old woman, especially when it involved telling her about her sister's part in the tragic years of bereavement.

Aunt Betsy. That, as well. There were too many people who had been touched by the tragedy of her making. Lilias, too, must believe herself bereaved, that her mother was dead, and buried in the cemetery here. I sat down at the still cluttered table, and tried to think.

If Davey's and my guess at what had happened was correct, then what would Lilias (I thought of her by name, as Gran had always spoken of her, rather than as the Mum of my childish memory) what would Lilias and her husband have done next, after their visit to what they thought of as Gran's grave? Gone back to wherever they were staying, and let Lilias take time to absorb the shock of her mother's death? Gone back to Iowa? Whichever, I had no way of tracing them. I leafed hurriedly through those pathetic letters again; there must originally have been an address, the one Aunt Betsy would have written to, but in the irritating American way, there was no heading to the letters, and the envelopes — deliberately destroyed, perhaps? — were not there. So, no direction except "Ioa"; no mention, even, of the respectable gentleman's surname. No way, in fact, for me to trace my mother.

What I suppose I hadn't sufficiently taken into account was that I, too, had suffered a shock. The events of the past two or three days, the confusion of the mystery, the sudden throwback into a forgotten way of life that nevertheless seemed to enfold me like a comfortable old coat, all these, I thought suddenly, must have addled what brains I had. Davey had seen it. I had only to think myself into Lilias's place, and it was obvious what she would do next.

She would look for me.

I found I was staring at the Unseen Guest. Or rather, clear through the picture and the metal door behind it, at what had apparently been the contents of Gran's safe. If in fact Lilias had taken the papers from the safe, had there been anything there from which she could get my London addresses — Jon's flat, or my place of work? I thought not. Gran, with the super-accurate memory of the semi-literate, would never have troubled to write them down, and my marriage-lines were in London. With a twist of wry amusement I realised that my mother was in the same boat as I was; she did not know my married name; could not, even, know that I had been married. She herself had spoken to no one in the village, and since I had arrived here after she and her husband had left, she must have no idea that I was due to come to Rose Cottage.

So what would she do? Come back to have another look at the cottage, to see if a more determined search would turn up a clue to her daughter's whereabouts? Possibly. It was more likely that she would try again to see the Pascoes. Even if, as it seemed, Aunt Betsy's letter had persuaded her that they had joined with the village in their condemnation of her, she might approach them now, with her husband's support, if her need to find me was strong enough. And so she would find out that I was here.

For the time being, then, I would have to stay. But as I put Lilias's letters back into the safe I wondered if, come morning, I would find myself wanting to dodge the issue. How in the world did one face a situation like this? The only precedents were on the stage, and even there domestic melodrama had been out of date for a long time, and had never had much connection with real life. There were no precedents. In actual fact, I thought, as I busied myself clearing the last of Gran's things off the table and packing them into the sideboard drawers ready for the removers in the morning — in actual fact there was as much sheer embarrassment as joy in the idea of such a meeting. What did one say? How act?" For both of us, the eighteen years would be a yawning gap, a gulf, both of years and experience.

There was a coward's way open to me. I would of course have to wait for the removers, but once the cottage was cleared I would be free to leave. Would it help both Lilias and me over a difficult moment if I just went? I could write to her, leave a letter here to break the news about the grave in the cemetery, and tell her of Gran's present whereabouts, and that we would both be waiting for her there at Strathbeg. I could send my heavy case back north with the removers, and, once they had gone, walk to the station and catch the five-fourteen train. With any luck I might be at Strathbeg before Gran's things got there . . .

Which was nonsense. A cowardly fantasy, dreamed up in the aftermath of shock. To do any such thing would be both stupid and cruel. Stupid, because even if I dodged the meeting here, I would have a possibly even more difficult one to face with Gran. And cruel to allow Lilias, who had come home to an empty house and (as she thought) the news of her mother's death, to come home a second time and find the cottage empty and stripped of furniture, and nothing but a note from the daughter who apparently did not want to meet her.

Telling myself sharply that I should be ashamed of even thinking about it, I wrapped up the last of the brass candlesticks, tucked it neatly into the drawer, and slid the latter back into place. It was no use trying to think what to do, what to say. Take the time instead to think what this meant to Gran, and what it would certainly mean to me. *Take life easy, as the grass grows on the weirs.* I had had my weeping time; this was a gift, take it as such, and take it easily.

I was half way up the stairs to bed before I remembered the other mystery that had been in the background all my life. The one person who would surely know the answer to that would be Lilias herself.

I went down and unlocked the front door, leaving it on the latch in case my mother should come home.

No one came.

No one, that is, until the morning brought Mr Blaney and Rosey with the milk, and the information that the removal van was already there, and waiting at the head of the lane till he was clear of it.

"You manage to get everything ready, did you?"

"Yes, just! I'll see you on Monday anyway, Mr Blaney, and I may be staying on a day or two after that. I'm still not sure of my plans."

He beamed. "There now! Wasn't I just saying the same thing to the missus? Once she's back here with her own folks,

I said, she'll likely stay a bit longer than she thought to. So if you're to bide for a bit, you'd like a couple of eggs again Monday?"

"I'd love them, thanks. Here's Rosy's biscuit. Oh, and the chicken was lovely. Would you tell Mrs Blaney?"

"I will, and you're welcome. She was saying it was good to have you home."

Rosy whirled him smartly up the lane, with the word almost echoing in her wake. Home.

The echo was dispersed, promptly and noisily, by the removers. They were cheerful, quick and reasonably tidy. Shortly before noon the big van backed cautiously away up the lane, and I heard the gears grind as she turned into the road and trundled off. I went back into the cottage and looked about me.

Home. A different echo now. The table was still there, and the four upright chairs, but the rocking-chair had gone, and Gran's fireside chair, and where the sideboard had stood there was its ghostly shape outlined in unfaded wallpaper festooned with dusty cobwebs. The mantelpiece was bare of its ornaments, but the fender was still there, and the fire-irons, and the cracket — the stool that had been my fireside seat as a child. The rug had gone, and the exposed edge of the lino in front of the fender was frayed and ugly. On the bare wall the shapes of the flying china ducks were like little ghosts.

Even a very minor move is somehow drastic. The place looked dead, and though I had done little through the morning except check with Gran's list and tell the men where to find the items that Davey had marked with the coloured stickers, I felt drained and depressed. At least, I thought, staring round me at the desolate remains of my home, it gave me something to do, a way to fill the waiting time. For my own comfort, as well as for Lilias's sake, I would do my best to get the place clean again, and at least reasonably comfortable.

But first, lunch. (Call it dinner, Kathy, you're home now.) Whatever it was called, it was a good meal, cold chicken and a tomato, with bread and butter and one of Prissy's peaches. I took my cup of coffee out into the sunshine and drank it sitting on the seat under the kitchen window.

The scent of Granddad's roses filled the air, and the beck ran sweetly over its washed stones. Birds were singing everywhere. It was very peaceful.

No one came.

I went in and started work.

At half past four I stopped for tea, reasonably satisfied. The floors were clean, the fire relaid, the exposed walls and skirting swept clear of cobwebs, and the windows bright. I went up to my bedroom, brought the bedside rug downstairs, and laid it in front of the fireplace. It was too small, and the colours had faded and worn to various shades of grey, but it covered the frayed edge of the lino, and was a distinct improvement. Even so, the room looked deserted and pathetic, with its bare walls and empty mantelpiece. I supposed that pictures and ornaments, even things like the brass candlesticks and the china ducks, gave life and spirit to the place, because they were someone's choice, they were loved. The Unseen Guest, which was still there, did very little to help. Home is where the heart is, and the heart had gone out of Rose Cottage. Soon, now, it would be a shell of its old self, waiting for the builders to "improve" it ready for its new tenants.

I still don't know what made me, at that moment, do what I did. There on the table beside me lay my pen and the writing-pad with the list for the removers. I tore the list off and threw it into the fireplace, then sat down and started to write a letter.

Not to my mother. To Lady Brandon. To ask if she would reconsider her plans for the cottage, and would either let it or sell it to me. I was still not too sure of my plans, I told her, but since coming back here I had realised that I would very much like to keep my old home. If she preferred to let it to me, I would do my best to put it in good order and keep it so, but I would really like to buy it. I would be very happy to let her see any plans I made for its improvement . . . and so on. I had not yet, I wrote, mentioned this to my grand-mother, but I would be coming back to Strathbeg soon and would, if her ladyship would like me to, come and talk to her and Sir James about it. I did very much hope that they would see their way to letting me have the cottage. I was . . .

I hesitated. I would normally have been theirs sincerely, Kate Herrick, but somehow the words weren't there. I finished the letter as I might have finished it ten years ago: *Yours faithfully, Kathy. (Mrs Herrick.)*

The signature was in its way an omen. I was a cottager again.

I looked up from addressing the envelope, my heart jumping. The garden gate had creaked.

Someone was coming up the path.

23

Not Lilias. Just Mrs Pascoe, coming in a hurry, carrier-bag in hand.

"Oh, Kathy! You've never been and done it all yourself! I meant all along to come and help clear after they'd gone, but I didn't think they'd be here so early. Ted Blaney said they nearly beat him to it."

"It's sweet of you, but there wasn't a lot to do. They were pretty good. There was only Aunt Betsy's room to clear upstairs. I shut the door on the others." I was watching for an indication that Davey had changed his mind and told her about our findings, but she gave no sign of it. She dumped the carrier-bag on the table and looked about her.

"Looks funny without the sideboard, doesn't it? She'll be glad to have her things round her again, though. She was always fond of that sideboard. Did you pack her tea-set, the one with the rose-buds?"

"Yes. Everything I thought she'd like, whether it was on the list or not. Did you come over from the Hall?"

"Yes. The men are real busy today. The plumbers have come — and not before time — and there's a lot to get sorted. Jim had to come home to pick something up, so I got a lift back with the van. They won't get home for their tea till late, so if there's any more clearing up to be done, I'll give you a hand. I brought my apron along."

"Thanks very much, but I've done all I mean to do, for the time being anyway. There's only Aunt Betsy's room to do up-stairs, and I've shut the door on that, too. I was just knocking off for a cup of tea, if you'd like one?"

"Never refuse a good offer," said Mrs Pascoe comfortably, "and here was I hop-ing you'd say just that. Here," fishing in the carrier-bag, "I've been baking, and I brought you some gingerbread. I mind how you always liked my gingerbread. And after tea, if you like, I'll turn your Aunt Betsy's room out for you."

"Well, thanks, that'd be great. Pretty nearly everything's gone from there."

"Your own room's all right? Davey did say you'd got all you need, but you know you're welcome to come up to us if it's more comfortable for you."

"Yes, he did ask me, but thanks all the same, I'll be fine here."

"You're staying on for a bit, Ted Blaney says?"

Ted Blaney seemed to have said rather a lot. "Yes. One or two more days, perhaps. I've no definite plans yet." I poured tea. "The gingerbread looks gorgeous. Fancy you remembering that."

"There's not much I could forget about you, nor about your poor mother either." She looked round the bare little room, and to my discomfort I saw her eyes brim with tears. She sniffed, smiled, and batted the back of a hand against her eyes. "There I am for an old fool. It's seeing the place like this, when it's been a friend's home for longer than I can remember." She drank tea, her eyes seeming to follow the flight of the shadowy ducks up the wall. "You're young yet, but you'll find it. You go through your life thinking things never will come to an end, but they do. It may be a comfort to those in pain, but it's a sore thing to know that things you've loved will be gone before you are."

"I'm sorry."

She set her cup down and turned to face me, dry-eyed now, but with some kind of strain showing in her normally cheerful, plump face.

"Well, I dare say that's why the good Lord gave us the gift of memory. But it comes hard. It was bad enough all those years ago when your mum left, poor lass, and she the nearest thing I've ever had to a real friend, but I never would have thought your Gran would go. I've been telling myself all this time that she'd be home, maybe, at the back-end, but dear knows there's nothing for her to come back for." A pause, but before I could speak she said, so abruptly that it sounded like an accusation, "And now you."

"Me?"

"Yes, you. Clearing the place out and then leaving."

"But I'm not leaving."

"Not for a day or two, you said. But that's not what I was meaning."

I smiled right into the troubled eyes, and pointed to the letter which lay on the table. "I've just written to Lady Brandon to ask if I may rent Rose Cottage, or better still, buy it. I hope she'll agree."

"Well! Well I never! That's good news, and I'm sure she'll jump at it. I know she didn't want your Gran to leave. You mean you're going to live here again, and maybe persuade your Gran to come back?"

"I don't know. It's just that I feel the way you do about the cottage. It's my home, and I don't want it to change or disappear. But there's something else."

"Oh? What's that?"

I set my cup down. The little click it made in the saucer seemed to finalise a decision already half made while Mrs Pascoe had been talking. If, as I had surmised, Lilias and her husband were to come back to Todhall and go to see the Pascoes again, Mrs Pascoe ought to be prepared for it. Even if our guesses were to be proved wrong, it was a mistake for Davey and me to keep our discovery a secret.

"There's something I have to tell you." I spoke slowly, wondering quite how to put it. "It's the reason why I'm staying on, at any rate for a time. Davey and I agreed not to tell anyone, but I think you and Uncle Jim should know. I'll have to wait and see how to break it to Gran." I pushed my cup and saucer aside and turned to face her. "Something happened yesterday that's changed everything."

She had been waiting with what looked like eagerness. The sad look had gone, so that I wondered if, after all, Davey had let out some hint. Her face lit to a delighted smile, and her cup went down into its saucer with a rap that could almost have cracked it.

"Kathy, dearie! I've been hoping! If you knew how I'd hoped! And when you came back, and things happened the way they did, I was sure. It's lovely news, lovely! But when did you — I mean, he's said no word to me?"

"We — well, we agreed not to." I hesitated, confused. "You were hoping? Do you mean you suspected something? But — for heaven's sake, how on earth did you guess?"

"Oh, I've known for long enough. He didn't need to say ought, but I'm his mother, and I've known all these years, and never a look at anyone else, let alone walking out with them, and I'll not soon forget what he was like when we heard you were married. He was on leave then, and that was the only time — it was Polly Walker from Fishburn, but it didn't last even till the end of his leave, though he might have done worse, she's a nice girl. Maybe I oughtn't to have told you, but I know you'll understand, and it's just between ourselves."

"Of course, but look, you've —"

"And then when we heard you were coming back here he — all of us — were afraid you'd have changed, and wanting different things and different ways —"

"Aunty Annie, please, it isn't —"

"And when I laid eyes on you I thought, no, he can forget it, but then you were just the same, for all you've been away so long, and I've been hoping, aye, and praying, too. I've missed your mother something sore, but now, maybe, with him and you settled here in Rose Cottage —"

"You've got it wrong," I said desperately.

"Listen, please! No, listen! It's nothing to do with — with what you think. I'm sorry. It's something quite different, not about me, or Davey, at all. It's something we found when we were packing Gran's things up yesterday. It's about my mother."

"About Lilias?" The colour had rushed up into her face as I spoke, but the last word brought her up sharply, her embarrassment forgotten.

"Yes. Davey found some letters upstairs in Aunt Betsy's room. They were hidden away. She may have meant to destroy them, but obviously she forgot, or didn't have the chance. I understand she was taken bad very suddenly at the end."

"That's so. But, letters? What letters?"

"Letters my mother wrote, and Aunt Betsy intercepted. And" — I swallowed — "this will be a shock, but not a bad one. I promise you, not a bad one. They were written, all of them, *after* the date when she was supposed to have died."

A staring silence. A hand up to her mouth.

"Supposed to?"

"Yes." I reached a hand across the table to cover one of hers. "She's still alive,

Aunty Annie. We're sure of it. And we think she and her husband have been here in Todhall recently, just this last week. I know" — as she started to say something — "I'm sure they'd have come to you, but it was last weekend, when you were away somewhere at a wedding."

"Wedding?" She was looking dazed. "Last weekend?"

"Yes. It's pretty certain that they came here, too; they would, of course, but they found the cottage empty, so they've gone, I've no idea where, but I think they're bound to come back to find some trace of me, and you'd be the person they'd go to, I'm sure. So you see why I had to tell you, and why I have to stay here myself till she comes, or till we're proved wrong?"

The flush had died from her face and she was very pale. She shook her head, not looking at me. "I can't get it. I can't see . . . Why? What happened? You say you're sure, but now you say you might be wrong? Kathy, love, you wouldn't say all this without you were certain, would you?"

"No. It's quite certain that she didn't die in that accident, and that's the main thing.

The rest is a guess, but it honestly looks like a good guess. She's been here, and if that's so, she'll be back." I got to my feet. "Look, just sit quiet for a minute while I make a fresh pot of tea, and then I'll tell you the whole thing."

The story was told, the questions, speculations, and exclamations over. We lapsed at length into an emotionally exhausted silence while the sun, wheeling lower, sent the shadows of the big trees stealing across the edge of the cottage garden, and my grandmother's "evening thrush" began his song from the top of the nearest elm.

Mrs Pascoe got to her feet. I must have looked as she did, tired but lightened, and moving as one does in a dream.

"I've got to go. They'll be finishing soon. I'll see you tomorrow, then. Whatever happens."

"Yes. Will you take this letter for me, please, and put it in the post? Here, you've forgotten your carrier."

"I reckon I'm not thinking straight yet." She sounded spent, her voice as flat as if she was talking about the week's groceries. "And I never did get to help you with the cleaning. There's that wicked old woman's room still to do. It can wait. I couldn't bring myself to lay duster to it after this."

"Forget it. I told you I shut the door on it. If I do buy the cottage I'll have to get the vicar to do a spot of exorcism. I wonder if he knows how?"

It was a feeble attempt to break the emotional tension, but it did the trick. We laughed, and then hugged one another — something we had seldom done — and she went to the door, pausing on the threshold to say, hesitantly, "I don't somehow like to leave you alone."

"I'll be all right."

"I ought to be at home anyway, in case" — that flush of joy again, this time for Lilias — "well, in case. But are you sure? Maybe I could ask Davey to come down — oh, no, maybe not." A pause, and then she went back to the question that still lay silently between us. "I got it wrong, didn't I? You and Davey don't have an understanding at all?"

"I'm afraid not."

"Then I'm sorry. I was hoping, and I let it run away with me. I can see it wouldn't be right for you."

I said quickly, "It isn't that. It just hasn't come up. I — I never thought about it. I had no idea he felt that way."

"Then for mercy's sake don't let him know I told you."

"Of course I won't!"

Another brief pause, then she suddenly reached up and kissed me. "Well, if it's not to be, it's not to be. But believe me, I'm as happy for you tonight, child, as I am for myself. Good night, and I hope she comes soon."

24

I scrambled eggs for my supper, and
ate Prissy's two remaining peaches. It was
a meal that took me back a few years,
eaten as it was on the bare table-top, and
with the "cooking" plates and cutlery
which were all I had kept out for my own
use. After I had washed up I did a lei-
surely tour of the cottage, ostensibly to
check that everything had gone that
should have gone, but in reality to do
something — anything — to occupy me
and keep my mind from turning over and
over in the same treadmill of speculation.

If we were right. If she should come. If
we were wrong, and no one came. If she
did not come tonight, then when? How
long to wait and wonder? If we were
right . . .

And so on. By the time I knew that I
had totally failed to fix my mind on anything else except the possibility of my
mother's return I was back in the kitchen,

where only the table and chairs and the Unseen Guest, along with the fireside tools and the cracket, remained to offer any kind of welcome.

Welcome? It looked, in the failing light, inexpressibly dreary. But it suggested something to do.

Flowers. That was it. Flowers, the loveliest ornament of all, guaranteed to charm any place to life. There was no vase to be had, of course, but a couple of Mr Blaney's milk bottles would do very well. Flowers and a bright, freshly lighted fire. No better welcome anywhere.

I found the bottles and rinsed them, leaving them ready in the back kitchen. Then I went out.

It was nearing nine o'clock, and dusk was drawing down. Behind the trees the first star pricked out, low and brilliant. The light breeze of day had dropped, and the evening was very still. The stream sounded loud. I walked down to the gate and stood leaning on the top bar, enjoying the scent of the roses, and straining to listen for any sound from the lane or the road beyond.

There is nothing that wakes memory so

quickly and vividly as scent. If my solitary supper eaten off the bare table-top had taken me back a decade or so, the fragrance of the roses took me back still further. Some of the bushes, I knew, had been in the old rosary at the Hall, which Sir Giles — the present baronet's father — had had cleared and replaced with the modern varieties that to his gardener were very much second best. My grandfather had brought a good many of the old bushes here to his own garden. Fashions had changed, in plants as in other things, and some of the roses were rare now, but not his favourite, the tough, ubiquitous old cottage rose that (if Davey and I were right) Lilias and her husband had dug up and taken to the cemetery for him.

If we were right. Back it came, the wearisome round of preoccupation. Would she come? Could we be wrong? And if we were right, then how, dear God, how to meet the situation? How cope with it?

Action again indicated. I went to gather the flowers, the still flourishing survivors of a season of neglect. There were lupins and irises, and some columbines soon to go wild, and, loveliest of all, the double white lilac that hung in scented clouds over the toolshed roof.

I was just about to make my way back to the cottage when I hear the sound I had been waiting for. A car turning in from the road and coming slowly down the lane. The toolshed was behind the cottage, so from where I stood under the lilac tree I couldn't see the lane or the gate. Nor could I see lights, though by now it was almost dark. I wondered briefly if it might be Davey, come down for some reason, but he would have used headlights, and this was a much quieter vehicle than the van. Clutching the flowers to me, I stood still, waiting.

The wheels stopped at the gate. The car door opened, and shut gently. Then came the click of the gate latch, and the squeak of hinges. Footsteps, almost inaudible on the weeds, but recognisably a man's, trod up the path. Then a tap at the cottage door.

I was just about to move to answer it, when I heard the door open, and after a moment, the sound of someone moving about in the kitchen.

The back window of the cottage, which

faced towards the toolshed, showed a crack of light; the kitchen door must be half open. My heart thumping, I moved forward and peered in through the window.

There was nothing to see but that crack of light, and the movement of shadow across it as the visitor crossed the room. A man's voice called, "Is there anyone there? Kathy?"

I pushed open the back door and went quickly through into the kitchen.

The visitor was a tall man, a total stranger to me, and he was standing by the fireplace, apparently examining the framing and stitchery of the Unseen Guest. As I entered he turned quickly, self-possessed and smiling.

"Well, hullo there! I guess you must be Kathy?"

I stared at him. Dark eyes, dark hair with a dusting of grey. Fifty years old, maybe; tall and thin, with skin tanned brown. American, by the voice and the clothes; light drill trousers, a casual, expensive-looking jacket, and a scarf knotted at the neck. He could have passed as a gipsy for Miss Linsey's "vision" at the graveyard, but more certainly he was my mother's respectable gentleman from Iowa.

I cleared my throat, but found myself unable to speak. I stood there, clutching the flowers to me, staring at him.

He spread both hands in a placatory kind of gesture. He might have been saying, "Look, I'm not armed." He spoke again, with a calming sort of social ease, obviously attempting to bring a bizarre situation under control.

"I hope you'll forgive me for walking in like this, Miss Kathy, and I'm sorry if I gave you a start, but I'm real I happy to meet you anywhere."

I found my voice. It came out none too steadily, and with no attempt at all at bridging the situation.

"Is she here with you?"

His brows went up, but he answered readily in that pleasant drawl. "She certainly is. She's right there in the car. But —" this as I started towards the door — "no, please! If you'll wait just a moment? I guess she's just as nervous as you are, so she asked me to come in first and see if you were home, and kind of break it to you. But it looks like I don't have to? You were expecting this? You know already?"

"Not know. Guess. You're Larry, of course?"

"I am. Larry van Holden. I sure am happy to meet you, Miss Kathy."

He put out a hand and, rather bemusedly, I took it. I was wondering how much, in the end, she had told him about me. "Make it Kathy. You're my step-father, after all." I turned back from the door and put the flowers down on the table. "All right, then. It's not just an easy meeting, is it? Perhaps you're right, it might be better to clear one or two things up before my — before we meet. I found it out only yesterday, that my mother was still alive, I mean, and that she'd married you and was living in America. It was when Davey Pascoe — she'll have mentioned the Pascoes? Yes? — well, when we were clearing Aunt Betsy's room to pack thing up for the removers, we found some letters, letters from my mother, hidden away. We worked things out from that, and from what we'd heard in the village, so we knew you'd been here. It was you who took the things from the safe in that wall, wasn't it?"

"It was." He hesitated. "I must tell you, we hadn't planned to visit here at all. It was my idea to come over to England, to look up traces of my mother's folks from north of here, near Hexham. The trip was a kind of holiday, and Lilias was two ways about it, a bit homesick, you can imagine, and wanting news of you and her mother, but being scared to come anywhere near the place in case she wasn't welcome. Then we saw something in a local paper, that the Hall here was to be made over, and this cottage fixed up as a rental, so Lilias began to wonder if her mother had moved away, or had maybe even died, and we hadn't heard a thing. So we came over — it had to be after dark so that no one would see her — and you know what we found. The cottage was empty, no sign of anyone, and poor Lilias — well, I don't have to tell you how she was feeling. So we went up to the village and she sent me to ask at the Pascoes" house, but there was no one there, so I went to the vicarage, and from what the girl there told me I took it that your grandmother had died, and your Aunt Betsy had gone back to her folks in Scotland."

"I knew about that. She said the same to me. 'The old lady died and the sister went back to Scotland.' "

"That's it. So we came back here. Lilias knew where the keys were, of course. No one had said anything about you being expected here. Lilias figured that your aunt hadn't know about the safe-cupboard, so she wanted to get the things from it, but we had no way of getting at it right then."

It was like coming alive again to feel that twinge of amusement. "Because the tools had all gone from the toolshed?"

"That's right. Why is it funny?"

"No reason. I'm sorry. Go on. You came back on Monday night?"

"That's right, we did, and we did our bit of safe-breaking. I've got the goods here." He dug into the pocket of his jacket and brought out a yellowed envelope which bulged with papers. He laid this on the table between us, and added to it, item by item, an assortment of small objects. I recognised Granddad's old turnip watch, the battered little box that held his medals and Gran's rings and the "Mizpah" brooch that had been his engagement gift to her.

I had been listening to his story with only half my mind; the other half was outside there, in the car at the cottage gate. The objects on the table, for so many days past an obsession with me, seemed quite irrelevant to what was happening now. I picked the envelope up, turned it over without seeing it, then put it down and opened the box. Two medals, a twist of paper holding five gold sovereigns, a thick old-fashioned wedding ring, a pretty, cheap-looking bracelet, a brooch of seed-pearls and peridots . . .

His voice said, gently amused, over my bent head: "They're all there. I don't know why I've been hanging on to them; we meant to leave them with your grandmother, but what with all that was going on there, I quite forgot. They've been in the glove compartment of the car."

I was hardly listening. I had picked up the bracelet. "But this?" I said. "This was sent back to Gran after the bus crash. It was on the — it was one of the things that identified Lilias. Her initials, see?"

"Yeah, I know. It certainly gave Lil a

shock to see it. She'd never heard about the accident, you realise that?" He took the bracelet from me and laid it back in the box. "This made it sure it was Cora and Jackie, their friends, who'd been killed. She'd given Cora the bracelet as a keepsake when they left. And they weren't the sort, any of them, to keep in touch, so they never knew."

"The travelling folk? I suppose not. But my mother did try. She wrote to us several times."

He was putting the other objects carefully back into the box. "She did, poor girl. So that's how you knew who'd been here, and how you found out about Lilias? You knew my name, even." He laughed. "You sure had me wondering just now if your grandmother had found the news too much for her. She promised to leave it to us to tell you, but I'd begun to figure that maybe she couldn't wait and had gotten herself to a telephone after all."

"What? *What did you say?*" The meaning of the quiet words, drifting past in that slow, even drawl, got through to me at last, and brought me up with a jerk. "Gran? What are you talking about? How would Gran know about this? I've never been in touch. What do you mean, Gran promised to leave it to you?"

"Just that. We've just got back from Scotland. That's where we've been since the weekend."

"Scotland?" I said blankly. "You mean you've been to Strathbeg?"

"That's right. When we left here on Monday night, thinking that Mrs Welland was dead, and that your Aunt Betsy hadn't troubled to let Lilias know, your mother was so mad that she just had to go straight up to Scotland to have it out, as we thought, with your Aunt Betsy, and find out what had happened to you."

"I see . . ." I took a long breath. "Yes, I do see."

I looked at him, at Lilias's rich, respectable gentleman, and, for the second time, found myself smiling. She'd have been upset enough, my poor mother, to face a dozen Aunt Betsys, and with Larry beside her she'd have found it easy. "It's a pity she didn't do it long ago!"

"It surely is. Poor Lil. All the way north in the car she was saying all the things she'd been wanting to say, and going over all the years . . . Well, she'll tell you herself, and it doesn't matter now, thank God, because when we got there, there was your grandmother, alive and well and not believing her eyes and ears." He showed a hand. "You can imagine."

"I'm not sure that I can."

"You can say that again. Well, I left them to it. I got to know that bit of Scotland real well in the hours I spent walking around the place while they talked. It's pretty, but kind of quiet, isn't it? And yes" — in answer to some questioning sound from me — "your grandmother's quite okay now, and she sends you her love and wants you back there just as soon as we can get you to go back north with us."

I didn't answer. I found I had sat down — collapsed, almost — into one of the remaining chairs, and put both hands to my face, as if the pressure on my forehead could steady the whirling confusion of thoughts and emotions. What did come with cool relief was the realisation that Gran's part in this was already played; she knew; she was happy, and according to Larry, well again. With that part of the tangle straightened out, the rest might not be so hard to deal with. What was left now was just between me and Lilias.

I found my voice at last. "It's wonderful. I — thank you for all you've done, Larry. It must have been, well, just wonderful for both of them."

He said mildly, "It was quite a scenario. But I reckon Lilias'll want to tell you the rest herself. Now look, this may be wonderful but it sure isn't easy. Are you okay?"

"Yes."

He went to the door and opened it. "I thought I heard someone — that's right, I did. There's a nice-looking young guy out there by the car, talking with her. I heard her laugh. She must be feeling better."

"It's Davey Pascoe. I thought he might come down. He's the son —"

"I know who he is. Well, that's great. There'll not be that much ice left to break, will there?" A kind look, as he paused in the doorway. "And I figure you can manage a bit of fancy skating if you have to. So what do you say I go talk to Davey, and walk about outside some more, while Lilias comes up here to you?"

25

There was a pause, while presumably he told her what had passed between us, then, while he stayed tactfully by the car talking with Davey, she came up the path alone.

I got up. I had not even been trying to think of what to say. There was no precedent for a meeting like this, save perhaps in some old Gothic tale. I steadied myself with both hands flat on the table, as she came up the path and paused in the doorway.

She would be a year or two over forty now, and the slender girl of the photos had put on weight, but I still would have known her, and she was till one of the prettiest women I had ever seen. On the fresh, lively beauty the pictures had shown, and the flyaway loving charm that I remembered, were superimposed the assurance of security, and the gloss of American grooming. A poised and beautiful woman, Lilias, even in the crudely lit and barely furnished cottage kitchen, the assurance, as she hesitated there in the doorway, did in fact seem a little fragile.

She stared at me, as Larry had stared, and then the smiles came, and with them the tears.

"Why, honey . . ." The phrase and the accent were recognisably American, but the soft voice was the same, and sharply, surprisingly, I remembered just how the dimple had come and gone, enchantingly, in her cheek. Remembered, too, the tears that had wetted my face on the night when she had kissed me goodbye.

"I — I thought you were dead," I said.

The dimple again, and she dashed a hand across herr eyes. "Darn it, I'm happy," she said. "I'm not crying. Well, I'm not dead, never was, but you — you might as well have been, and Mother, too, but now — for goodness' sake, we ought to be rushing into each other's arms, but we'll skip that bit till we know one another better, shall we? Just say hello?"

She came into the room, still with her eyes fixed on me. "Yeah, well, he said you were a beauty, and you are." The little trill of laughter that, out of the past, I remembered. "But not a patch on your mother, he said, so how's that?"

"What I'd expect," I said, smiling back. Her light handling of the situation was making it easy. "It's hard to know what to say, isn't it? It's all come as such a shock, everything suddenly happening, coming right . . . I'm happy, too, but I don't quite know what to say, except that I'm so terribly sorry we lost you like that, and lost all those years, but it wasn't our fault, Gran's and mine."

"And don't I know it! Don't fret yourself, Kathy love, Mother and I got it sorted out, what that old witch had done, and now Davey's been telling me how you'd got it worked out yourself from some letters of mine you found in her room." A sideglance. "I suppose you had to read them?"

"Yes. I'm sorry." I was still, rather helplessly, feeling around for what to say. "But we had to. I didn't know anything, you see. And it was so marvellous to find we'd been wrong all the time, even though it had been done in that beastly way. It was you and Gran who had the worst, I know that. I was just little, and I missed you terribly, but children get over things. But even so — all those years — to be without you . . ." It broke from me with the force of anger. "How could she? How could anyone do what Aunt Betsy did?"

"Jealousy," said Lilias, wisely. And looking at her, lovely, still young, beautifully dressed, moving with her graceful walk round the shabby kitchen, looking about her, touching here and there, as if to help her remember, it was easy to see how she could have wakened a hell of resentment in a narrow and barren heart. She said over her shoulder, "Take it easy, honey. It's over, and we're here, and there's a lot of life left for us all still."

"I know. It's okay. But it's hard to take. It's easy to see why she would want you out of the house, but once you'd gone, to cut you off, deliberately like that, from me and Gran, and for good — " I took a steadying breath. "Poor Gran. What did she say when she knew?"

"After the bells of heaven had stopped ringing and we came back to earth and thought about what had happened?" A smiling slant of the head as she lifted a corner of the cotton curtain and examined it. Her eyes came back to me, and were suddenly grave. "I'll tell you exactly what she said. I'll never forget it, and nor will Larry. She just said, 'Poor Betsy. She thought she was doing right, keeping sin away from Kathy, and trouble away from me. She was a good woman, Lil dear, in her way. Try to remember that.' " A look where mischief mingled with a kind of ruefulness. "When I told Larry, you know what he said? 'Then may the good Lord preserve me from good women!' " And the gravity broke up into the delicious laughter. "He has, too, and don't you and I know it!"

In spite of everything, I found myself laughing with her. "Do you mean that your respectable gentleman from Iowa — I read your letters, remember? — still doesn't know about — well, the truth about me? I've been wondering just where he thought I came in. He didn't seem surprised to see me."

"We knew you'd be here. Mother told us." She picked up a spray of lilac from the table, and was silent for a moment, brushing the scented flowers to and fro across her mouth. Above the white blossom the lovely eyes regarded me, I thought warily. "No, I know what you mean. Okay, you'll have to know. He thinks you're Jamie's daughter."

"I see."

She said quickly, "I didn't actually tell him that, but I know that's what people said at the time, and Jamie and I did get married later, so it was a fair guess, and I just let it be. The rest — of course I told him — well, maybe not everything, but most of it. He knows why I left home, and about that letter, the one Aunt B wrote, and why I was scared to come home, even though I wanted so much to see Mum again, and to find out about you." A pause. "I know that was the worst thing I did, leaving you, but with the kind of life I knew I'd have with Jamie, unsettled, I mean . . . well, it was best for you, the way I was thinking then. And I did mean to come back, if things changed, but it didn't work out that way. You do understand, don't you?"

"Yes."

"And you have to believe that I never stopped thinking about you, and Mum, and Rose Cottage . . . It's true. Larry guessed it, too. I truly think that's what he planned this trip for, not really to go back to his own family's roots at all. He's — well, it was something to me to find that people can be good, real strict with morals, I mean, and still be so kind."

"I'm glad. And of course I believe you. I could tell from the letters what it meant to you to be cut off from home."

"I reckon I'll have to see what was in those letters. Where are they?"

I nodded a head towards the Unseen Guest. "In the hidey-hole."

"Well, what do you say we light the fire and burn them up? I've got the key here in my purse."

She turned quickly away to the fireplace and reached up for the box of matches as if she had put it there herself only yesterday. She struck a match and stooped to set a light to the fire, then stayed there by the hearth with her back to me, watching while the paper caught, and the kindling burned up with a pleasant crackling blaze. Evasive action, I knew, but I could find no words for what I wanted to say, so I waited in silence, watching her as she watched the flames. She turned at length, but without meeting my eye, to pick up her handbag, which she had left on the table, but before she could open it I said, "Don't bother. It's not locked. Davey and I broke the box open."

"So you did. He told me. I forgot."

"Mother — Mum —"

It came out hoarsely, and I stopped.

"Make it Lilias, can't you? We're the same age now, and believe me, likely to stay that way!" This time the light tone didn't ring quite true. Her attempt at a laugh trailed away, and we stood there awkwardly, one to either side of the table, looking at one another.

I found my voice. "Never mind the letters. We've got to talk about it, you know that. I've got to ask."

"Ask what?"

"You know what."

"I suppose so."

"It wasn't Jamie, was it?"

She did not answer straight away, but pulled out the nearest chair and sat down at the table facing me. She seemed to do it in slow motion, as if approaching some barrier which would take calculation and then painful effort to surmount. Her face, which had been slightly flushed from stooping close to the fire, was pale again; paler, I thought, than before. For the first time I could see the faint, give-away lines that strain had sketched near eyes and mouth.

I found that somehow I, too, had sat down.

She was regarding her hands, folded together in front of her. Then she looked up to meet my eyes.

"No, honey. It wasn't Jamie."

"Then — please — ?"

Colour came up in her cheeks again, making her eyes look very bright. She shook her head, and then said with the slightest quaver in her voice, "I know. I know. I have to tell you. You've enough to forgive me for already, but now you're going to have to forgive me all over again. You see — that is — darn it, I don't know how to start!"

I said abruptly, "Was it Sir James?"

That brought her upright in her chair, looking so shocked that, nervously keyed as I was, I wanted to laugh.

"The master? What an idea! Of course

it weren't!" It might have been the pretty house-maid of twenty-odd years ago, scandalised and protesting. Even her voice had slipped its careful accents. "How could you think such a thing? He wouldn't never — ever — have dreamed of it, and neither would I! That would have been a real disgrace! Oh, no, it was — there was no harm in it — or so we thought." A pause, and then, as memory came back, a hint of her enchanting smile. "I was only sixteen, don't forget, and he wasn't much older, your father, I mean, though somehow I never think of him that way. It was all quite innocent in its way."

"Then why have you never told anyone, Gran or me? Is it because it's somebody awful?"

"Give me some credit!" Another flash of the pretty Lilias, and this time I certainly saw the dimple flicker. "As if I'd ever — oh, well, I'm afraid — what I mean is — what I'm trying to tell you is, I know you've a right to know who your father is, but the truth is, I don't rightly know myself!"

That really did knock the breath from me. I tried for words, and only managed, crudely, "What do you mean, you don't know? Do you mean there were so many of them?"

"Give me some credit!" she said again, and now I was sure of the dimple. "Of course there weren't, not that could have been your father, I mean! I don't say I didn't always have plenty to choose from, but he . . ." She leaned forward, gravely earnest now. "You have to believe me! He was the first, and then the only one till Jamie. By the time I knew I'd fallen wrong — though that's a silly way to put it, since having you was the best thing I ever did in my life — he'd gone, and I didn't want to chase after him and maybe make a peck of trouble, and, well, there was no point to it. Do you see?"

"I — I suppose so . . ." I said awkwardly, then, on a rush, "but no, I don't see. How could I? If you've never wanted to get in touch with him again, neither Gran nor I are likely to try. So if he was your only, well, your only real lover, then why won't you still tell anyone who he was?"

"Because — oh, it all sounds kind of crazy now, but I swear it's true. Okay, I'll try to tel you how it was." Her hands fluttered, palm out, sketching a gesture of surrender. "That summer — I still remember every minute of it! It was gorgeous that year, and they seemed to have parties all the time at the Hall. Every weekend, seemingly, the place full of young folks, and cars, and tennis and dancing . . . You've never known what it was like in them — in those days. People had house parties, and dances, and there was always lots of young folks at weekends, and *fun.* It was such fun!" Wistfully. "And in the servants' hall we had fun, too. Oh, it was a lot of work, but nobody minded that — and of course the tips were good."

A pause. I didn't speak. After a few moments she went on. "I was house-maiding there, you know that. Well, one night when they, the gentry, were all at dinner I went up to help turn the beds down and carry the hot water — you had to do that in those days — and when I went into his room he was there. He hadn't gone down to dinner. He hadn't even started to change. He was just sitting on the bed in his shirt-sleeves with a letter in his hand, and he was crying."

Another pause, then she went on with the story.

It really was, as she had said, an innocent one. The young man — a boy of perhaps eighteen — had come back from the day out with the other guests to find that a letter had come with the afternoon post. It was from his mother, breaking the news to him of the death of his dog, at thirteen years old the beloved companion since he could well remember. The old dog had been run over by some brute who had driven away and left it to die in the road. His mother had given no details, but the agonising end could be guessed at, and his distress had left the young man quite unable to face the company downstairs. The rest followed naturally. He had tried to hide his tears, while she, in all simplicity offering what seemed natural comfort, had run to put her arms round him and try to soothe the grief away.

They said side by side on the bed while he talked, and later she contrived, unseen, to get a tray of supper up to him. And the acquaintance thus begun had blossomed. Next day — her afternoon off — he had met her with his car at the end of the lane to Rose Cottage, and they had spent the rest of the day together. After one or two snatched meetings during her working days at the Hall, he took to driving down after dark through the Hall grounds to wait by the wooden bridge, and Lilias, whose parents went early to bed, found it easy to creep out to meet him.

"He stayed three weeks," she said. "Then we said goodbye and he left. I suppose we would have said we were in love, but we both knew there was no question of getting married, and we both knew it would never have done. But we had a lovely time together, and *liked* each other, as well as being romantic, if you know what I mean. And it was a couple of months after he'd gone before I knew about you coming, and another few weeks before I dared tell Mother and Dad, and there'd have been no point in trying to chase him up and make trouble, and in any case he'd told me that he was trying to get a job abroad somewhere. India, I think, or Australia. Somewhere like that. So you see?"

"Yes." It was somehow not a conversation one could have had with the mother who had brought one up, but we were, as she had said, on a level. Certainly I could not have asked the question that had been suggesting itself to me, irresistibly, as she told her story. "And are you going to tell me that I started life in the back of a car?"

She looked shocked, then she giggled. "It was a two-seater. There's some details you don't have to have! But if you want to know, it was probably up there in Gipsy Lonnen." A lift of the shoulders and a little laugh that told of tension relieved. "Oh, I knew I'd love you again, even with all the time lost, and all the changes!" She took in a long breath, and let it out in a sigh. "Oh, well, it's all a very long time ago, and if you're the wages of sin, Kathy love, all I can say is, it was worth it!"

There was another pause, then for the first time she made a move to touch me. Her hands came out, and mine went to meet them. She said nothing, but it was in answer to something unsaid that I told her,

"It's all right, it is, really."

"If you knew how I've dreaded this! It was the only good thing about being cut off from the family, but I knew I'd have to come back some day and get it over with.

I've told you all I can, but look, Kathy, if it matters so much to you, there are ways of finding out the rest, what happened to him, I mean."

"No," I said. "I'm glad you've told me this much, of course, I am, but I'd rather not take it any further. I mean that."

It was the truth. I felt nothing but relief, the lifting of a vague dread that had nagged me ever since I had come back to Rose Cottage. And I had spent the first ten minutes or so of the interview wondering if I was going to hear that my father had been some married man with a reputation and career to lose, or one of the visiting chauffeurs who hadn't cared to take the responsibility of a child. It came like a burst of sun clearing the mist away, that it didn't matter either way.

I smiled at her, and repeated it. "It doesn't matter at all. I think you and Gran and Granddad were right about that. I couldn't have had a better home or better folks than I did have, except for missing you."

That brought the tears, and with them at last the kisses and the final relief of spent emotion. Only for a minute or two, then my mother, recovering herself, reached for her purse and started on repair work, while I retreated to the fireside to tend the fire and dab my eyes dry unseen.

Still kneeling by the hearth I watched her for a few moments, then said, uncertainly, "Look, I'm sorry, but we can't leave it quite yet. Why did you say you didn't remember everything? We've agreed to do nothing about it, okay, but really, this is one thing I do have a right to know. *Who was he?*"

She sat back in her chair, while a look compounded of mischief, embarrassment, and sheer irrepressible amusement brought the sparkle back to her face.

"I only meant," she said, "that I don't remember his name."

"Lilias!"

"I know, I know! But it was such a long time ago, and in some ways it's gotten that it's not much more than a dream. All I remember is that he was handsome, and he was a real sweetie, and he stammered a bit when he was excited, and he had a red sports car with a copper exhaust pipe and a strap over the hood, and everybody — me, too — called him

Bunny, but I think — I'm pretty sure — that his name was George."

Five seconds or so of complete silence, then I laughed.

Not quite the "proper" reaction, perhaps, and there may have been a touch of hysteria there at this ending to my long search, but it was a good ending, and, as I was fast discovering, I was my mother's daughter. So I laughed, in reaction, relief, and because it was funny. *Take life easy.*

Lilias stared, gasped, then giggled, and suddenly all was well, very well, and the lost years, the Aunt Betsy years, were past and done with, and the future was ours. America, Strathbeg, Rose Cottage, it didn't matter. It was ours.

My mother sat up, dabbing her eyes again. "Oh, Kathy, honey, I love you . . . ! Darn it, I've got the hiccups now! Just let me put my face right again, and what do you say we tell poor tactful Larry and your handsome Davey to come in, and for godsake is there a kettle around here some place, and have you any tea?"

26

There was, and we had, and I boiled the kettle and found some cups, while Davey shifted the chairs to the fireside and pulled the cracket forward to act as a side-table, then followed me through to the back kitchen where I was hurriedly pushing the flowers into the milk-bottles and a couple of the remaining slices of bread into the ancient toaster.

"Okay?" was all he said, and I nodded.

"I came down just in case. You don't mind?"

"Of course not."

"He seems a nice chap, the American. Easy to get along with. Seems he has a big business, selling property. Real estate, he called it. That's all we talked about, really, and cars. That's an Armstrong-Siddeley he's hired, and he's quite keen on it. I thought you'd like to know."

"About the Armstrong-Siddeley?"

"Don't be daft. You know what I mean."

"Yes, I know. It's all right, Davey, I'm all right. It went — it was okay."

He still lingered. "Kathy?"

"Mm?" The first two slices popped up and I put two more in and started the buttering.

"What d'you say I go home and tell my folks that she's here and it's all okay? Since you talked to Mum this afternoon she's been like a cat on hot bricks, wondering if it's all real. Can't rightly believe it."

I stopped buttering to consider it, knife in hand. "Better still, why not bring them down? It's getting late, and I doubt if Larry and Lilias plan to call anywhere else tonight, and they're going back north tomorrow. Tell you what, ask them, but I think that'd be great."

It would also, I couldn't help thinking, as the toast went on popping and I went on buttering, help to spread the burden, leaven the lump, whatever metaphor meant "make the situation less close and overloaded with emotions".

While the last two slices were toasting I carried the flowers through to set them on the mantelpiece, to find that Lilias, who had been reading the letters retrieved from the Unseen Guest, was making a kind of laughing ceremony of consigning them to the flames. But as the papers blackened and wisped away up the chimney I, from where I was by the mantelpiece, could see a faint reflection of the firelight on her cheek, as if a tear had spilled there. She caught my eye and smiled, then dusted her hands together and said, gaily, "There! That's the past disposed of, Kathy love, and the future to drink to. And in English tea!"

And presently, with tea and toast — the toast I would have had for my breakfast — the three of us settled round the fire with a fair assumption of cosiness, and put together what was left of the story — those parts of it which could, with Larry there, be told.

My story had to come first. Gran had told Lilias about the missed years of my girlhood, and what she could about my marriage with Jon and its rough ending on that April night over Pas de Calais. Later, I supposed, my mother would want to know more about those whirlwind months, but now she kept to easier topics, my life since that time, the London job, my home there and my friends, and what I thought of Todhall where, like Larry in Hexham, I was "rediscovering my roots."

This brought us home to Rose Cottage, and I had to tell the story of my house-to-house detective work, and my attempts with Davey to unravel the mystery. Lilias, half amused, half wistful, plied me with questions about the village and the people I had talked to, unconsciously betraying what Larry had told me about her homesickness. He, listening half absently, as if to some fairy-tale, sat smiling, with his eyes on his wife's face, and — I noticed — leaving his tea untasted.

When I told them about Miss Linsey and her gipsy ghosts my mother laughed, and sent a sidelong look at her husband. "A gipsy? Well, I suppose he could be. They say you always fall for the same type, don't they? I'm Larry's third, and the other two were both blonde."

"And beautiful," said Larry, giving her the sort of fondly admiring look that Americans find it easy, and Englishmen impossible, to bestow.

Then it was America's turn, and I heard

about Iowa, and their home there, and the two daughters ("sweet girls") who were both married now and lived not to far away; and this in its turn led to invitations and promises. I must go to Iowa and visit with them; in fact why wouldn't they take me right back with them when they left? I could make it right with my boss in London, surely? They had originally meant to fly back this next weekend, Larry told me, but it could easily be put off. He himself had to be home by the beginning of July, but if Lilias wanted to stay on, and maybe bring me back with her . . . ? But in the meantime I obviously could not stay here in this half-empty cottage, so, since they had promised Gran to drive straight back to Strathbeg, and take me with them —

"Tonight?" I said, startled into stupidity by a vague memory of American hustle during the war.

But no. Tomorrow. Tonight they would be going back to their hotel. Not the one in Corbridge, where they had been staying while Larry hunted up his Northumbrian ancestors; they had called there on their way south and had telephoned ahead to book into a hotel in Durham.

"The Three Tuns, it's called," said Larry, "and I'm told that Durham's only about nine miles from here. When I called them I said we might be pretty late, but they'll hold the rooms. For you, too, of course."

"Well, thanks very much, and of course, I'd love to go to Strathbeg with you, but if you don't mind, I'd rather stay here tonight. I've still got — well there are things to do, and . . . would it be all right with you to pick me up here tomorrow?"

I think he would have persisted, and I would certainly have found it hard to explain my reluctance to leave the cottage for the comforts of the Three Tuns, but I was saved by the noise of the Pascoes' van coming down the lane.

Lilias, jumping to her feet, ran to the door and opened it.

"Annie! Why, Annie!"

"Lil!"

They flew together, and the rest was lost in a flurry of greetings, and along colloquy, mostly in whispers, held half way up the garden path. Then, both talking at once, they came back into the kitchen, with a grinning Davey in the rear. He pulled up an empty packing-case that the removers had left behind them, set it beside me and sat down on it.

"Your father," I said, "isn't he here?"

"No," still grinning. "He knew how it would be. Let them get it out of their systems, he said, and come and tell me about it later on. They'll be back, he said, and that'll be time enough. He takes life easy, my Dad."

"Like you?"

"I try. So what's the plan?"

"They're going to stay tonight in Durham, and drive back to Strathbeg tomorrow. They want me to go with them."

"Will you?"

"Yes. Apart from everything else, I'd like to be there when Gran's furniture arrives, though that's the least of it now! Larry did want me to go with them straight away, but I thought I'd like to stay here tonight. It's all a bit sudden, and a bit late, if you see what I mean."

"Yeah, I do. Sleep on it before you pull the roots up?"

I said, surprised, "That's exactly it."

"And you're going to? Pull them right up, I mean?"

I had been wondering if his mother had

told him about my bid to buy Rose Cottage, but this answered me. As I hesitated over my reply I was saved yet again by an interruption from outside. Davey had left the door open — the fire, while providing cheer, had made the kitchen rather too warm for the June night — and outside in the dusk I heard again the creak of the gate. Someone was coming up the path.

I saw my mother, who was near the window, turn to look out.

"Who on earth's this? Some woman, with a shopping-bag?"

"Oh, heavens," I said, "it's Miss Linsey!"

"So it is! Larry, quick, look, that's the witch who saw us in the cemetery! The one Kathy's been telling us about. What on earth does she want here at this time of night?"

"Goodness knows" I said, as I went to the door. "Miss Linsey! How nice! Won't you come in?"

"Oh, Kathy, I hope you don't mind my coming at this hour, but I've been rather worried, and I did just wonder — oh!" as her eye went past me to take in the rather crowded kitchen. "You've got company. I didn't know. I thought you'd be on your own, and so I came down — " A scream, as Larry hose from his chair.

"That's him! There you are! I knew it was true! That's him! That's the gipsy!"

"And me," said my mother. "How are you, Miss Linsey?"

"Lilias Welland!" Another screech from Miss Linsey, as she thrust her shopping-bag at me and surged forward to seize my mother's hands. "I knew it was you! I told them you were coming back, and no one would believe me! They said you were dead, and I knew it wasn't true! I've seen you so many times in dreams, and then I saw you in the cemetery —"

I missed the rest. As the kitchen filled with a babel of talk and exclamations the shopping-bag wriggled in my hands and I screamed, too, and dropped it on the floor. Something shot out of it, and up the curtains to the rail, where it hung, fizzing. A kitten, small, tabby, and furious. It balanced there, glaring down at the scene.

"She's brought her familiar," said Davey in my ear, just as Miss Linsey, still clinging to my mother's hands, said over her shoulder, "I brought it for you, dear. It's one of Patsy's, and quite clean. I found homes for the others, and I meant to keep it, but it can't stand Henry, so I thought of you. Since you'll be staying here at the cottage I thought you might like the company."

"Well, thank you, it's very sweet, and I'd love to have it, but what made you think I'd be staying here? As a matter of fact —"

"It was my dream last night." The light intense gaze turned on me. "So I knew. I saw you here, it was Rose Cottage, I knew it, but it wasn't the same. There was — " a vague glance round at the denuded kitchen — "well, there was some furniture, and it looked as if —"

I saw her catch sight of Davey and she hesitated. I heard Davey say "Oh, no," under his breath, and, as she opened her mouth to go on I put in, quickly, "I'd love to keep the kitten, if someone can get it down from there! I'm going away tomorrow, as it happens, with my mother and Mr Van Holden. This is Mr Van Holden, my step-father. Larry, do meet Miss Linsey, one of our neighbours."

Larry shook hands, making gently courteous noises of greeting, and inquiries after her health, which, mercifully, turned her attention to him.

"You sound like an American. I met one during the war, and of course there are the films. I didn't know they had gipsies in America?" Indians, of course, and ho- boes, or do I mean bozos?"

A choking sound from Davey, and I saw hysteria in his eye. Lilias, over at the win- dow trying to entice the kitten down from the curtain-rail, stiffened, peered out at the dusk-filled garden, and clutched at my arm.

"Jumping Jesus," she whispered, but with complete reverence, "look there! Isn't that the other two from Witches' Corner? I'd know Miss Mildred anywhere, and Miss Agatha is surely wearing the same old hat." She turned to Larry, who, I could see, was making a great hit with Miss Lin- sey. "Larry, love, we seem to be holding a convention. More neighbours. The call- ing hours have changed some since I lived in Todhall, and will you for God's sake see if you can get that kitten down?"

Larry, reaching up from his six-feet-plus, detached the kitten gently, hook by hook, from its hold on the curtains, and lifted it down to a perch on his shoulder as I hurried to the door again. "Miss Agatha! Miss Mildred! How nice to see you. Do come in."

"It's not too late, is it?" began Miss Agatha, and Miss Mildred, pushing past her sister, leaned forward to say in a whisper, "Is she here? Is Bella here?"

"Yes. She came just a few minutes ago."

"Oh, you've got company." That was Miss Agatha, looking past me, as Miss Linsey had done, at the thronged kitchen. "There, you see, Millie, I told you it would be all right. There really was no need to fuss."

I must have looked puzzled, because Miss Mildred hurried to explain. "The thing is, my dear, Bella's been rather tiresome today, going on and on about things, you know how she does, and then she said she was coming down to see you again. Well, I thought you were on your own, and I was afraid she would upset you, even though you said it didn't bother you, all her talk, so I thought I'd come and see."

"I told her you had too much sense to let Bella's nonsense upset you," said Miss

Agatha, "but she insisted, so in the end I came with her —"

"But with all these people here —" added Miss Mildred.

"It was quite unnecessary after all," finished Miss Agatha."

I said warmly, "It was sweet of you, Miss Mildred. Both of you. But everything's fine. More than fine. Won't you come in? There's somebody here who'd love to see you again."

27

It was Mrs Pascoe who saved the situation from getting completely out of hand. Pushing Davey and me in front of her, she herded us into the back kitchen.

"Now, Kathy, I know what's bothering you, and you needn't worry, nobody's going to say anything they shouldn't in front of Mr Van Holden. Whatever you may think of those ladies, they *are* ladies, and it's not likely they'll say anything that might give Lil a red face. So that's that. Now, where's the wine, Davey? I knew you wouldn't have any here, Kathy, so I brought a bottle along, to celebrate. It's my own elderflower champagne, and this was a real good batch. If Davey'll get it open, we can give them a glass each, and then we'll drive them home. That'll get rid of them with no hard feelings. I think you and Lil have about had enough."

"Good idea," said Davey, producing the

bottle. "Okay, Mum, this should fettle them. Get the glasses, Kathy."

"No glasses," I said, rather shakily.

"There's some jam-jars out in the tool-shed. I saw them when I stole the tools."

"Behave yourself, Davey," said his mother. "Take no notice of him, Kathy. Come on, I'll help you rinse the cups out."

"Hold up, love," said Davey, to me." No, don't tell me, you haven't got a cork-screw?"

"You wrong me, every way you wrong me, Brutus. That's one thing I have got." I had kept one back for Prissy. That pleas-antly civilised lunch seemed a very long time ago. I routed it out, and while Davey wrestled with the cork Mrs Pascoe and I hurriedly rinsed out the tea-cups. We did not quite have to descend to jam-jars, as Larry, still clutching the kitten to him, qui-etly materialised beside us with a couple of elegant tumblers from the picnic basket in his car. These, with my tooth-glass, al-most made up the quota, and Davey made do with a small, and it was to be hoped clean, jar that had once held fish-paste.

I saw that my mother, abandoning hope,

had gone down under a wave of delighted chatter from Witches' Corner. If she had been afraid of some drawing aside of skirts among the Todhall neighbours she need not have worried. All parties seemed to have plenty to say, and said it at length, and all at the same time. Davey determinedly broke it up, wading in with the wine, which was received with pleasure, and then Larry, tea-cup in hand and kitten on shoulder, somehow got silence, and, standing there in front of the dying fire, prepared to make a speech.

"Well, now ladies — and you, Dave — I am not going to make a speech. I am only going to say — Dear God!"

A fascinated pause as the kitten launched itself from his shoulder to the mantelpiece, by way of the top of the Unseen Guest. Larry, to the intense admiration of everyone present, simply reached a long arm, retrieved it, and held it to him while he went calmly on not making a speech.

"I would like to say," he said, "how very much my wife and I appreciate the welcome we have gotten here in Todhall. We have had the most warm and loving welcome from our lovely daughter, and now from all of you here tonight. It has been a great pleasure for me to meet you all, a very great pleasure. It's getting late, and Lilias and I will be to be going soon, but we'll be back here, never fear, and we'll hope to see you all when we visit again, as we certainly have plans to do. This darned cat has about sixteen claws to each foot. What are you going to do with it, Kathy?"

"Keep it, of course."

"But if you're coming with us tomorrow —" began my mother.

"We'll look after it for Kathy till she comes home," said Mrs Pascoe. I saw Lilias glance quickly at her, then at me, but she said nothing.

"You'll really keep him, then?" said Miss Linsey. "I'm so pleased. I do love them to get a good home. What will you call him, Kathy?"

I smiled at them all. My mother and her dear respectable gentleman; Miss Linsey, the true prophetess who had seen what I knew to be the future; the other witches, beaming kindly at me over Larry's picnic tumblers; Mrs Pascoe, who shared my secret. And Davey. With a sudden lift of the heart, I raised my tooth-glass in the toast.

"I'll call him George. Here's to George!"

"To George!" echoed everyone, and drank their wine down. My mother was smiling mistily, looking very happy and, though I could see she was exhausted, as pretty as a picture.

Then one saw how she managed it. After one long, assessing look at her, Larry took charge. He handed the kitten over to me, then somehow, without seeming to hurry them at all, he had the three witches, taking cheerful farewells of me and the Pascoes, shepherded out of the kitchen and down the path towards the big car. My mother hung back, with a whispered word to Mrs Pascoe, then turned to say good-night to me.

"Till tomorrow, then, sweetie. Isn't that wonderful? Till tomorrow."

A few more words and a kiss, and then she went, but slowly, to stop half way down the path and look back, as if to commit the scene to memory, the dim garden, the ghost of the white lilac, the shadowy bulk of the cottage with me standing in the lighted doorway. Then she went, and the gate creaked shut behind her.

As Larry settled her in the car Mrs Pascoe said, "We'll have to go too. The van's in their way. You'll have to back it up, Davey." Then to me, "You know that letter you gave me to post?"

"Yes."

"I brought it back. It's in my bag here. I thought, if you're going up to Strathbeg yourself, maybe you'd rather talk to Lady Brandon when you get there? She was on the phone just before we came down, and it was to tell me that they'd had an offer for Rose Cottage."

"Did she?" That was Davey. "Were they planning to accept it?"

"What's it to do with you?" His mother was dismissive. "Go and shift the van, Davey. He's got the car turned already."

"An offer for Rose Cottage?" I was surprised at the force of my dismay. So short a time it seemed since my own hopeful net had been cast into the void. "But surely she'd never sell without telling us? Did she say if Gran knew?"

"Yes. She approved."

"But who on earth would Gran approve?"

"Me," said Davey.

We both turned to stare at him. His mother's hand went to her mouth, and she said nothing. He smiled at me.

"So you see it's got quite a lot to do with me. I was going to ask you about it, Kathy, but I didn't reckon on being rushed into it like this with half the village looking on and Mum rabbiting on about moving the van." He put out a hand and touched, not me, but the kitten, so that it purred and clung and butted its head into my neck. "I'll have to go. But I'll be down here early, before they come for you, and — maybe I can ask you then?"

"I'll be here," I said.

They have gone. Silence came back, broken only by the sound of the stream and the purring of the kitten in my arms as I walked down to the gate. The scent of Granddad's roses filled the air. An owl called from among the trees in the Hall grounds. Another answered, breathily, from somewhere in Gipsy Lonnen.

Gipsy Lonnen, where it had all begun.

Well, I knew now. As much as I would ever know. As much as I wanted to know.

Take love easy, as the leaves grow on the tree.

I would try. The quest, in the end, had been for myself, and I had been answered. It isn't the roots that matter to life, it's the flower. No more questions, no more looking back. I had found myself, and I knew where I belonged. I was part of this place, and it was part of me. It was home.

I still had the tooth-glass in my hand, with a little wine left in it. I raised it towards the dim looming of the treetops at the head of Gipsey Lonnen.

"Whoever you were, and wherever you are, may God bless you, George," I said.

The kitten, no doubt assuming that I meant him, purred.

16